"I had nothing left."

Natalie took a deep breath for courage and looked Colt in the eyes.

"When I got out of the hospital I was up to my eyeballs in debt and barely able to walk." Just talking about it brought it all back. The fear. The sorrow. The hopelessness. "And then I went out to the barn to see Playboy. I wrapped my arms around him and buried my head in his mane and I knew that somehow, someway, I'd ride him again."

She felt the familiar burn of tears in her eyes. He started to move past her again, but Natalie snatched his hand and tugged him toward her, silently begging him to understand with her eyes.

"I'm sorry," she admitted, holding his gaze. "I don't expect you to understand..." She squeezed his hand and then turned to leave. But something changed.

One moment he was immovable, cold. The next he'd pulled her up against him and dipped his head down toward her.

With his thumb, he brushed away a stray tear on her cheek. "I do understand."

D0043931

Dear Reader,

It's no secret I love horses. As a child I used to read books by Marguerite Henry, gobbling up tales of Misty and Stormy and Justin Morgan. I firmly believe reading provided early training for my career as an author.

I can't tell you how proud I am to be a writer. It's a dream job for someone like me—someone who loves to read. I call myself the author of grown-up girl horse stories. Each one of my books features the animals I love. Sometimes those stories are light on horses, sometimes they feature more prominently.

Her Rodeo Hero is one of my personal favorites. Perhaps it's because it's not about horses as much as it's about a woman who's been injured by one and her fight to get back in the saddle. It's also about a man with his own scars, one whose love of horses helps him to conquer inner demons and find a love of his own.

I hope you enjoy *Her Rodeo Hero*. I loved rereading it during the revision process, something that doesn't happen as often as you might think. When it does, it's usually a sign of a good book. I hope you think so, too. And I hope Marguerite Henry is proud.

Best,

Pam

HER RODEO HERO

———

PAMELA BRITTON

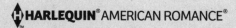
HARLEQUIN® AMERICAN ROMANCE®

If you purchased this book without a cover you should be aware that this book is stolen property. It was reported as "unsold and destroyed" to the publisher, and neither the author nor the publisher has received any payment for this "stripped book."

ISBN-13: 978-0-373-75586-8

Her Rodeo Hero

Copyright © 2015 by Pamela Britton

The publisher acknowledges the copyright holder of the additional work:

A Home for Christmas
Copyright © 2005 Laura Marie Altom

Recycling programs for this product may not exist in your area.

All rights reserved. Except for use in any review, the reproduction or utilization of this work in whole or in part in any form by any electronic, mechanical or other means, now known or hereinafter invented, including xerography, photocopying and recording, or in any information storage or retrieval system, is forbidden without the written permission of the publisher, Harlequin Enterprises Limited, 225 Duncan Mill Road, Don Mills, Ontario M3B 3K9, Canada.

This is a work of fiction. Names, characters, places and incidents are either the product of the author's imagination or are used fictitiously, and any resemblance to actual persons, living or dead, business establishments, events or locales is entirely coincidental.

This edition published by arrangement with Harlequin Books S.A.

For questions and comments about the quality of this book, please contact us at CustomerService@Harlequin.com.

® and TM are trademarks of Harlequin Enterprises Limited or its corporate affiliates. Trademarks indicated with ® are registered in the United States Patent and Trademark Office, the Canadian Intellectual Property Office and in other countries.

Printed in U.S.A.

www.Harlequin.com

CONTENTS

With more than a million books in print, **Pamela Britton** likes to call herself the best-known author nobody's ever heard of. Of course, that changed thanks to a certain licensing agreement with that little racing organization known as NASCAR.

But before the glitz and glamour of NASCAR, Pamela wrote books that were frequently voted the best of the best by the *Detroit Free Press*, Barnes & Noble (two years in a row) and *RT Book Reviews*. She's won numerous awards, including a National Readers' Choice Award and a nomination for the Romance Writers of America Golden Heart Award.

When not writing books, Pamela is a reporter for a local newspaper. She's also a columnist for the *American Quarter Horse Journal*.

Books by Pamela Britton

Harlequin American Romance

Rancher and Protector
The Rancher's Bride
A Cowboy's Pride
A Cowboy's Christmas Wedding
A Cowboy's Angel
The Texan's Twins
Kissed by a Cowboy

HQN Books

Dangerous Curves
In the Groove
On the Edge
To the Limit
Total Control
On the Move

Visit the Author Profile page
at Harlequin.com for more titles.

HER RODEO HERO

Pamela Britton

In memory of Troy Parke, a man who embodied the word *hero*. The world lost an angel on earth when you passed away, Troy. You are missed.

Chapter One

Amazing.

Natalie Goodman watched from the grandstands, mouth slack, as Colton Reynolds stepped back from the black gelding, lifted his arms and gave the cue for his horse to rear one more time.

"See." Jillian Thacker, one of Natalie's best friends, leaned in toward her. She had to yell to be heard over the appreciative roar of the crowd around them. "What did we tell you?"

The gelding pawed at the air, mane flying like a royal banner, nostrils flaring. The horse was clearly listening to Colt's commands—or did it watch for them? Natalie couldn't tell.

The man in the arena seemed a mysterious figure in his black hat, black jeans and black shirt, a conjurer come to ply his trade with a magic wand. The only thing missing was a cape to complete the image. A day's growth of razor stubble covered his square chin, but the rest of his face remained in shadow. Yet something about the man's stance told Natalie all she needed to know, just like last time. She'd met him once before, at a wedding. She hadn't been impressed. Today she couldn't look away as she watched him lower his arms. The horse's front feet returned to solid ground. The crowd that lined the rodeo arena went wild again.

"He's the real deal, Natalie." Jillian's fiancé, Wes, tipped forward so he could peer around Jillian, his handsome face glowing with approval. "If you're looking for someone to help train your horse, he's your man."

Train her horse. Because she couldn't. Or shouldn't. Doctor's orders—no more horses. But Jillian and Wes didn't know that; they thought she only needed help to learn a new sport. They had no idea she'd been forbidden to ride, period.

"The trouble is getting him to agree," Wes added.

That didn't surprise her. The time they'd met he'd been about as friendly as a stepped-on dog. That was before, back when she'd been one of the top riders in the country, slated to represent the United States in international competition. She'd had her whole career mapped out, and then… *Bam!* The wreck. The recovery. The restructuring of her life. She'd lost everything but her sense of determination.

She refused to think about that. Instead she focused on her surroundings inside the Arroyo Grande Rodeo Grounds. The sky had blossomed a deep blue this morning, and a few wisps of fog had floated through a field of bonnets. The crowd let out a gasp of surprise as Colt's horse suddenly bowed, its nose touching the ground. Natalie hadn't even seen the man give the command. Nor did she see him signal for the horse to get back up and then head toward an open trailer parked in the middle of the ring, one with Colt's name emblazoned on the side along with the words Rodeo Misfits in an Old West–style font.

"I've seen him take some of our rescue horses and turn them completely around…" Jillian had to wait to finish because the crowd had erupted again when the black gelding climbed into the horse trailer without so much as a by-your-leave from Colt. "He's a miracle worker."

A year ago Natalie wouldn't have believed that the day would come when she'd need help training a horse. A year ago she'd been riding high after winning a silver medal at the Pan American Games. A year ago she hadn't been recovering from the worst riding accident of her career.

A lot could change in a year.

"Does he train professionally?" she heard herself ask.

Jillian's black bob brushed her cheeks as she shook her head. "No."

If Natalie didn't miss her guess, her friend's eyes lost some of their luster. "He's a bit of a recluse, but Wes can bring him around."

"You hope."

"No. He will." She smiled and clutched her fiancé's forearm. Wes tipped back his straw cowboy hat and gave his wife-to-be a kiss, after which Jillian said, "Wes and Colt go back a long way."

Natalie hated the thought of asking anyone for help, especially a reluctant someone, but desperate times called for desperate measures. "Okay. Let's do it."

Was that relief she spotted in her friend's expression, too? She hated to admit it, but it probably was.

Jillian had been present when she'd attempted to ride her horse without a bridle the first time, something that might seem crazy, but was actually an emerging sport. To say it hadn't gone well was an understatement.

Down in the arena Colt waved to the crowd, the white bucking chutes behind him contrasting starkly against his black attire. Natalie thought the act was over, but she was wrong. Just as Colt went to swing the trailer door closed, the black horse came bolting out. She thought the animal had made a mistake, but something about the way Colt acted, the way he placed his hands on his hips and then shook his fist at the animal, told her that this, too, was part of his skit.

Sure enough, the animal came barreling back toward him, and the crowd gasped yet again when it seemed as if the horse might run him down. It didn't. Instead the animal snatched a black handkerchief, something Natalie hadn't spotted before, out of Colt's back pocket and ran off with it. Colt spent the next few minutes making a big show of trying to get it back, much to the crowd's amusement. Natalie continued to be amazed as the animal expertly played its part. Finally, Colt appeared to give up. He climbed into the driver's seat of his truck, pretending to be so mad he'd decided to drive off with the trailer door still wide open. Natalie saw why a moment later. As he drove out of the ring, the black gelding followed, leapt for the open door, and then whipped around, still holding the black handkerchief. The horse waved it at the crowd as if saying goodbye.

"Amazing," she heard herself say.

"He is." Jillian and Wes applauded as loudly as the

rest. Heck, even the cowboys who sat or stood behind the chutes gave him a hand. "Wes can go down and talk to him right now."

Natalie stood up. "That's okay."

Jillian's pretty green eyes dimmed. "Are you certain? Colt would never so no to Wes."

She smiled tightly. "He won't say no to me, either."

DAMN SPURS. THEY ALWAYS seemed to hang up in the carpet of his truck, Colt thought. He'd nearly fallen on his ass when one of the rowels snagged a loop as he hopped out. He'd be glad when he could take them off. He never used the damn things anyway—they were all for show. Part of the act. Jeans, black chaps and black cowboy hat. City people seemed to expect that.

"Get on out of there, Teddy."

The gelding stood just where he expected—at the back of the trailer, head hanging out, handkerchief still clasped in his mouth.

"Come on. Show's over."

He could swear Teddy understood, because the horse dropped the handkerchief, lowered his head to examine the ground before gingerly stepping out of the trailer—looking for all the world like a toddler exploring new surroundings for the first time—and came over to Colt. Soft puffs of breath emerged from the black muzzle as Teddy attempted to sniff out the treat he knew Colt would have stashed somewhere. Finding which pocket was part of the game, and it didn't take the gelding long. Within seconds he was nuzzling Colt's left hip, darn near knocking the halter Colt had hanging on his shoulder to the ground.

"Peppermint." Colt reached into his pocket for the

treat, unwrapped it, and offered it to the horse. "Your favorite."

The gelding suckled the mint as if wanting to make it last. It made Colt smile. He fingered the wrapper, thinking back to the time when he couldn't even get near the creature. That'd been two years ago and there'd been days when he'd been ready to throw in the towel, but he hadn't given up. The horse wasn't the only one with an abusive past. He understood more than most what it took to overcome that kind of adversity.

"We got you turned around sure enough, though, didn't we?"

"You sure did."

Colt looked past the horse and right into the eyes of the most beautiful woman he'd ever seen.

Scratch that.

He'd seen her before, at Zach and Mariah's wedding, and he'd done a double take back then, too. He'd noted the blue, blue eyes. The heart-shaped face and wide lips. The only thing different was her thick blond hair. She'd cut it off. Still no makeup, though. Women as attractive as she was didn't need anything to help them look better.

"You're—"

"Natalie Goodman," she finished for him with a small smile.

"That's right." It wasn't like him not to look at a person directly, but for some reason he couldn't maintain eye contact with this pretty blonde. "English trainer or something," he said, slipping the halter on Teddy.

His friend Wes had mentioned her a few billion

times. Wanted them to meet, thought they'd get along, yada yada yada. His friend didn't understand. Beautiful or not. Animal lover or not. Smart or not. Colt wasn't the relationship type. Never had been, never would be. His past was just too…messy. Military. Crazy dad. It'd all left a mark. Things never worked out, and that was okay. He didn't need anybody or anything. Just his horses.

"Hunters and jumpers."

He peeked back at her. She smiled even wider. He patted Teddy's head. "Well, nice to see you again, Miss Natalie Goodman. I hope you enjoyed the show."

With any luck, she'd leave. She didn't. He glanced over at her again. Off-white shirt—peasant blouse, they called it—and skin tight jeans. Too good-looking for her own good. He didn't think he'd made a good impression the first time they'd met, and judging by the way one side of her mouth lowered, he would bet he wasn't earning any bonus points now.

He began tying Teddy to the trailer. "Something I can do for you, ma'am?"

"Actually, yes." She forced the wattage of her smile back up a notch. "I need a favor." But her grin was as precarious as a butterfly perched on the edge of a flower, and an instant later it slipped, that sweet face of hers rearranging itself into an expression of resignation. "Wes and Jillian suggested I talk to you."

Colt could well imagine what was behind that suggestion, considering the number of times Wes had hinted at getting them together. He forced himself to look her full in the face.

"What kind of favor?"

"I need a horse trainer."

He had to have misheard her. "Sorry?"

She took a step toward him and brushed her short hair over an ear, almost as if she'd forgotten for a moment that it wasn't long anymore. "I need a trainer. Someone who can make horses do things I can't."

Teddy nudged him, almost knocking him over, reminding him that he'd been in the process of tending to the horse. Wasn't like him to lose focus like that.

"Sorry, but I must be slow on the uptake. From what I've heard you're the best thing since sliced bread. Horsewoman of the year. International fame. What could you possibly need me for?" He lifted a brow. "Thinking of chucking it all and starting your own rodeo company?"

The side of her mouth tipped upward again, the beginnings of a smile, a *real* smile, brightening her blue eyes. "Something like that."

He finished tying up Teddy. He really didn't have time to sit around and chat. He had to get on the road fairly quickly if he wanted to be up north before dark. He had a show in Sacramento tomorrow.

"So?" He bent to check one of Teddy's front feet. "Do you have a problem horse or something?"

"I have a problem life."

He set down Teddy's foot. *Join the club.* "Okay, spill."

Oddly, or maybe not so oddly since he made his living watching things closely, he found he could read her like a book. He spotted the way her desire to ask for help warred with her sense of independence. She didn't really want to be there, standing in a parking area for rodeo competitors, talking to *him*.

"I've decided to take up a new discipline of riding." The grin she wrestled onto her face didn't seem to want to cooperate. "Freestyle reining, preferably without a bridle."

He'd been about to cross to Teddy's other side. Instead he froze and looked at her from beneath the angled brim of his cowboy hat. "You're kidding, right?"

"Nope."

"What—did jumping lose its appeal?"

She looked down to the ground, but not before he caught the subtle flinch. "I need a change."

Need? Not want? "And you can't make that change yourself."

It wasn't a question, more like an affirmation of facts, but she didn't seem to like the words because her head swung up. "Reining seems pretty straightforward compared to what I used to do, but in order to be competitive, I need help. And riding my horse without a bridle isn't coming along as quickly as I'd like. I need someone to tell me what I'm doing wrong. Shouldn't take you more than a visit or two."

"Why do you want to ride bridleless?"

She lifted her chin. "Because it's the most amazing thing I've ever seen. I want to master it."

And he'd always wanted to fly jet planes. Didn't mean it would happen. "That can't be done in a visit or two. Teaching a horse to trust you, to listen to you out of love and not because you demand it, something like that takes time."

"I've got all the time in the world."

"But I've got a full schedule. This time of year, summer, is my busiest season. I'll be lucky to be home three days this month."

"Could you spend one of those days with me?"

He almost laughed. Did the woman not understand? He spent most of his life on the road. The last thing he needed was one more thing to do when he managed to get home. "Not without rearranging a lot of stuff."

"Just one lesson."

He shook his head. "I told you. One lesson won't be enough."

"Then two. I'll pay you for your time."

"Don't you have enough to do with your jumping career?"

Direct hit. Disappointment poured from her eyes. Disappointment and sadness and resignation. She tried to hide it, or maybe even to ignore it, but it didn't work.

"I can't jump anymore." She tapped her head. "Bad wreck last year, right after Zach and Mariah's wedding. I almost died." She broke the connection of their gaze for a moment, clearly battling memories. He watched her take a deep breath before meeting his gaze again and saying, "I lost all my clients, had to sell the horses I jumped, gave up the lease on my riding facility. When I got back on the one horse I still owned it was like learning to ride all over again. I can train people on the flat, from the ground, and I have a few new clients now, but nothing like I had before. I need to keep all four feet on the ground—all four hooves, that is. No more jumping. It's just not physically possible for me. So here I am, starting over, and reining is what I want to do."

Don't do it, he warned himself. *Don't you get sucked in by pity. Or a pair of pretty eyes.*

"You really think you'll never jump again?"

The chin tipped even higher. "I told you. Never."

He glanced at Teddy. Though he told himself not to go down that road, he found himself wondering what he would do if he were told he could never perform with his animals again. If he was forced to stop doing the thing he loved, the thing that was his sanity. His calm in the storm of life. His saving grace.

Damn it.

"I can maybe give you one or two nights this month, *if*—" he stressed the word with an index finger "—I'm in town."

"Oh, thank you!" She took a step forward. He knew what she wanted to do, and he stepped back just in time. The move stopped her cold, and it also brought puzzlement into her beautiful face.

"I'll call you when it looks like I'll be back." He untied Teddy and headed for the rear of the trailer.

"Do you want my number?"

"I'll get it from Wes."

She nodded, her smile bursting forth like the sun over the horizon. "You won't regret this."

Too late, he thought as he loaded up his horse. He already did.

Chapter Two

The one good thing, Natalie thought, the only bless-ing, was that she'd found some new clients recently. Granted, they were all at a backyard barn in a not-so-good part of Via Del Caballo, but she'd given it her all and had been rewarded with half a dozen 4-H kids and a few adults.

No more million-dollar horses. No more big-ticket clients. No more fancy riding facility.

She tried not to think about that as she groomed Playboy, the horse she'd bought a few months before the accident. It was only by the grace of God, and a lot of help from her friends—Wes and Jillian, Zach and Mariah—that Natalie had held on to the gelding. Despite what she'd been told about the future of her riding career, she'd refused to give him up. Every-thing else had been sold to help pay medical bills.

Stop thinking about it.

She heard tires crunching on gravel, turned away from where Playboy had been tied to a single rail hitching post, and spotted Colt's fancy black truck with all his sponsor logos splashed across the front. It looked out of place when he parked next to her beat-up Ford F250, like a new shoe sitting next to an old one. There were days when she definitely missed her previous truck, Lola. She watched as he glanced over at her vehicle, no doubt wondering why she drove such a jalopy. He was parked in front of an old lean-to stall, one with tattered fencing that had once been painted white, but was now more brown than anything else.

"Is that the guy?"

Laney, one of her 4-H kids, a girl with more passion for horses than half a dozen of the spoiled brats Natalie used to train, paused in the middle of mucking out her horse's paddock. This was a self-service facility. No more grooms to take care of everything.

"That's him."

"I looked him up on Google last night," Laney said, her blond ponytail sliding over one shoulder. "Did you know his dad was some kind of rodeo cowboy, too? He used to be really famous. Performed in movies and everything. Colt took over the family business."

Yeah, if rodeo clowns could be famous. Not that Colt was a clown. Not really. A specialty act, they called it, and he was good. That's what she needed to remember if she were ever to perform on the back of an animal again. If she ever wanted to hear the roar of the crowd and feel the pride that came from being united with a four-legged creature, Colt was her only hope.

"Wish me luck," she said to Laney.

"Can I watch?"

"Sure. Why not?" Maybe the two of them would learn something together.

Colt had spotted her. He'd pulled up not far from

where she'd tied Playboy. He gave her what seemed like a half-hearted wave.

"Here we go," she softly told the gelding, stepping back and eyeing the horse objectively. He'd changed a lot in the year and a half she'd had him. His once mousey brown coat now had dapples. His mane had gotten longer, too, and he'd grown. He was nearing sixteen hands. Big for a Western horse, but she was nearly five-eight and he fit her perfectly.

If she could learn how to ride him again.

"Nice place," she heard Colt say as he slipped out of his truck.

It wasn't a compliment and it immediately got her dander up. "It's affordable."

She glanced around, trying to stem the flow of embarrassment that threatened to overcome her. Two years ago she would never, *ever* have considered keeping a horse in such a ramshackle facility, now here she was. Two years ago she would have stuck her nose in the air at the lean-to fencing, dirt road and uncovered arena. Not anymore.

"I bet." He tipped back his cowboy hat. "But is it safe?"

Was he purposely trying to make her feel bad? It'd taken forever to get him out to the ranch. He'd handed her one excuse after another, and she'd resorted to calling Wes and begging for his help in the end. That had done the trick, but she wondered if Colt resented her forcing his hand.

"I went over every square inch of Playboy's pen." She patted the dark bay gelding's neck. "I spent days cleaning out all the old muck. And another day replacing old boards. It's in as good a shape as possible."

Colt must have realized he'd offended her because he softened his gaze. "I'm sure you did."

Her nerves made her edgy. And irritable, too. She hated that she'd had to ask for help. Hated that she was in some backwater barn working with a cocky cowboy who clearly didn't want to be there any more than she did. At times such as these she ached for her old life with a ferociousness that left her feeling sick.

"This is Playboy," she said into the silence. Well, as silent as a horse stable could be. In the background a horse nickered. Chickens ran wild. Off in the distance you could hear the sound of cars from the nearby interstate.

"Nice-looking horse."

It smelled at the Lazy A Ranch, too. Not like pine shavings and saddle soap like her old place. No. More like horse poop and wet dirt. The other owners weren't as good at mucking stalls as she was. As she and Laney were. She glanced over at the young teen, sure she was listening to every word.

"I bought him at the Bull and Gelding Sale last year. The one up in Red Bluff."

He moved close enough that he could place a hand on Playboy's neck. She saw it then—kindness filled his eyes as he leaned toward the horse. It took her by surprise, that look. It reminded her of her friend, Jillian, when she "spoke" to animals.

"Is he cutting bred?"

Colt's gaze lightened as sunlight angled beneath his cowboy hat and caught his eyes. Hazel. The kind that turned green, gold or brown depending on his mood. He had the square-shaped face of a comic-book hero and the muscular build of a navy SEAL.

Something about him commanded attention and she couldn't figure out if it was his height, his broad shoulders or his piercing eyes. He stepped back, scanning the horse up and down like a used car salesman would a vehicle.

"He is. A kid trained him before me. I figured he must have a pretty good mind if he'd let a little boy break him."

"What have you done with him?"

She tried not to let her embarrassment show. "Not a whole bunch lately. I was flat on my back for a while, but when I climbed back onto him last month he seemed to remember everything I'd taught him." She was the one who'd had problems…still had problems. Balance. Vision. Equilibrium.

"And you tried to ride him without a bridle?"

His look seemed to say it all. And, okay, maybe it hadn't been one of her best ideas.

"Before my accident I was riding him every day," she said in her own defense. "He was listening to vocal commands and everything, but when I took his bridle off, he seemed to forget everything."

"Let me guess." A small smile came to his face. "Runaway pony."

"Something like that."

She hoped he didn't see the momentary flare of remembered panic that came to her eyes. She thought he hadn't, but then, just as quickly as it'd arrived, his grin faded away.

"How'd you get him stopped?"

"I had a friend in the arena with me."

He crossed his arms. He wore the same black outfit as before, right down to the hat, and she wondered if he'd come straight from a rodeo performance. It was the weekend and late enough in the afternoon that she supposed it was possible.

"You mind me asking why you picked reining? Surely Western pleasure would be better?"

She'd asked herself the same question at least a million times. "Have you ever seen freestyle reining?"

"I've seen a lot of things."

"Then you know what it's like. Breathtaking. I was hooked the moment I saw a video on YouTube over a year ago. It's like pairs ice skating or synchronized swimming or a ballet performance. Your horse becomes your dance partner. You, the music and your animal. Dancing."

She couldn't see his eyes beneath the brim of his cowboy hat, couldn't see if he understood. If she hadn't known better she would swear he was hiding his gaze from her.

"It's going to take a lot of work."

"I'm not afraid."

"Then let's get started."

ONE LESSON.

He'd said the words over and over again on the way to the Lazy A Ranch. He absolutely didn't need a project, especially a female project and her horse. He had his own baggage to deal with—the ranch, all the repairs, his full rodeo schedule.

"Should I saddle him up?" she asked.

"Nope. We're going to do some groundwork first."

She glanced over her shoulder toward the young girl behind her, the one who tried not to be obvious about listening as she diligently cleaned her horse's stall. The same spot she'd been cleaning the entire time.

"Do you mind if Laney watches?"

"Nope." Colt glanced around. "This place have an arena?"

"It does." He thought he heard her mutter, "Sort of."

He glanced down at Natalie, sunlight reflecting off her short hair. She waved her young friend over, completely oblivious to the way he studied her. It had occurred to him earlier that her hair might be short because of her accident, and his friend Wes had confirmed it. She'd been wearing a helmet when she'd had her wreck during that jumping competition, but it'd been cracked clean in half. Video of the accident showed she'd been stepped on after the horse had flipped over on her. There'd been talk that she'd never ride again. Clearly she'd proven her doctors wrong, but just the thought of it, of what she'd been through, made him shudder. Wes said she had a scar on her head. Colt had scars, too, although his were mostly on the inside.

Don't be getting soft.

One lesson. He had a busy life and he preferred to live it on his own schedule.

"So what are we doing?" Natalie asked.

"I told you, ground work."

"I've already done all that."

"Not this kind."

"You going to teach Playboy how to bow?"

"Nope." His dad used to teach his horses how to do that. But as Colt thought back to the methods dear old Dad had used, the way he'd tie a rope to a horse's front leg, forcing it forward while at the same time pulling down on the halter—not just any halter, but one with metal staples in it—he resolved yet again never to treat his horses that way. Ever.

"Do you need me to go get a lunge line? I still have a surcingle, too."

She'd stopped outside what he presumed was the arena, one with sagging boards and dirt footing. The wooden gate didn't look as though it would open, and if it did, that it wouldn't stay on its hinges for very long. It was rimmed by ramshackle wooden shelters and sad looking horses—like their own equine audience. Crazy. He suspected it wasn't really an arena. More like a dirt patch everyone used because there was no place else.

"He's wearing all he needs."

The hinges held, miraculously, and the kid Natalie had signaled to earlier leaned against the top rail of a fence stripped bare of paint. Surprisingly, it didn't collapse beneath her weight. Someone really should spend some money to fix up the place, he thought. He would swear they'd used recycled garage doors to make the horse shelters.

"Okay, now you've got me curious," Natalie said.

"Go on and walk him forward." He watched her for a moment. "Now stop."

She did as asked, and just as he expected, Playboy took three or four steps past her.

"Make sure to say 'whoa,'" he called out. "Do it again."

She repeated the process one more time, only this time she used her voice. Didn't help. The horse still moved past her.

"He's not listening to your verbal commands."

"Yes, he is. I'm barely pulling on the lead rope."

"He should be stopping the second you do. Not one second later, and especially not two. Right away. Bam." He slapped his palm. "He has to be listening to not just your voice, but your body, too. Once you're in tune with each other, he'll be able to read the direction of your eyes. You'll be able to tell him which way to step with just a slight tip of your head."

"He'll follow my eyes?"

"He will. I'll give you some exercises to help him with that, but we'll start on the ground. Trot him out for me."

She stared at him oddly. "Trot?"

"Up the middle of the arena."

"As in run alongside of him?"

Why did she stare at him so strangely? "Yeah, that's generally what one does when one trots a horse."

She shifted her weight to her other foot. "Okay."

She ran like a three-legged moose. He couldn't believe it. She seemed so lithe and svelte he would have sworn she'd move like a ballerina.

"I don't jog too well."

She was out of breath and clearly embarrassed. That was an understatement. "We'll need to work on that."

"I'm sorry." She sounded so sincere, so genuinely contrite that it made Colt feel like a jerk. She might run like a drunk, but she was still beautiful. Still in need of his help. Still clearly desperate.

"Good thing you already know how to ride."

Her chin ticked up a notch. "I can do better."

"Okay then. Let's try it again. Be sure to use your voice. Tell Playboy to stop."

She did as he asked, and maybe she ran a little more gracefully this time, but it was hard to tell.

"I've never really been good at running," she admitted after a few more attempts. "Maybe there's another exercise we could try?"

There it was again—the apology. She really was trying. Even so, Playboy had a hard time reading her body language with her wobbling this way and that. Worse, after watching her a few times, Colt realized this wasn't going to be one lesson or even two. She would need someone to teach her grace and fluidity, something he'd assumed she already had. That meant training. He might even need to ride her horse himself. That would mean interacting with her a lot more than he'd expected, and something about that made him uncomfortable.

Son of a—

This changed everything…and not for the better.

Chapter Three

Colt hadn't looked happy. He'd given her three more exercises to work on and then left. Natalie wasn't certain he'd ever be back.

"Damn."

She watched his truck make a left out of the boarding stable's driveway.

"Did you know he's performed in front of royalty?"

Natalie turned to Laney, curious despite her disappointment. Once again she reached to shift her long hair over her shoulder, but it wasn't there. It was like losing a damn limb, having her hair chopped off. She swore she'd never get used to her short-cropped locks.

"He has a website." Laney held up her cellphone as if expecting Natalie to read the screen herself.

"Really?"

Laney couldn't hide her excitement. "I stumbled on it while he was working with you. He has, like, all kinds of pictures and stuff on it. Did you know he's a regular at the National Finals Rodeo? And that he's a saddle bronc rider, too? He took over the family business when he left the military. He was twenty-six when he left the Army to help his dad, and four years later it's more of a success than ever."

Saddle broncs? That explained the cowboy swagger. And, yes, she'd known he was something of a big deal in the rodeo world—Wes had made that perfectly clear—but for some reason she'd been under the impression he'd done the rodeo thing for his whole life. Military? She'd had no idea.

"Next time he comes out here I'm, like, totally going to get his autograph." The teen continued to peer down at her screen. "He has printable fan cards. I'll bring some out here for you and me."

If he ever came back out again. To be honest, she didn't have much hope of that, and the admission caused the sick feeling to return. It was the same sickness she'd felt when he'd asked her to run alongside her horse.

"Come on. You can help me put Playboy away."

Laney jumped to the task so quickly it brought a smile to Natalie's face. She reminded her of Kate, one of the grooms she'd had at Uptown Farms, back when she could afford to pay someone to help her. Rather than fill her with bitterness, though, the memory served to firm her resolve. She wouldn't let Colt quit on her. She would overcome her physical ailments. She had to.

It only took a couple of phone calls to find out where Colt lived, although her friend Jillian cautioned against dropping in on him. Natalie ignored her friend and two days later set off on a field trip of sorts. It dawned a perfect day for a drive. Blue sky—the kind of blue that only happened after a recent rain—so crystalline and vivid it seemed Photoshop had lent God a hand.

She pointed the truck toward a section of town where she'd always wanted to live, only she couldn't, not even back when she could afford pretty much anything she wanted. Situated at the base of the mountains that separated the town of Via Del Caballo from the ocean, the land along the bowl-shaped valley had been owned for generations by ranchers. Parcels rarely became available in the low-lying foothills covered year-round by grass and majestic valley oaks whose branches brushed the ground. It took a half-hour to get out there, and as she approached she could see the Santa Ynez Mountains looming in the distance, as barren and brown as the valley was soft and green below.

There were so few driveways out to the east that it was easy to spot Colt's, but even if she'd been in doubt as to whether or not she had the correct address, the sign above the entrance would have made it clear. An iron oval bearing the words Reynolds's Ranch were suspended between two telephone poles, and below it stood a pair of ornate black gates, each with an *R* cut into it.

Jillian hadn't warned her about this. Should she climb over? But she had no idea how far the ranch was from the front gate and all she could see from her vantage point were spotted pasture and old barbed-wire fencing.

She pulled out her phone and texted Jillian.

You don't happen to know the pass code, do you?

What pass code?

To the electronic gate.

What gate?

I'm at Colt's ranch, sitting outside the front entrance.

If her phone had been a cricket it would have been chirping into the silence. Clearly, either Jillian didn't approve, or she didn't know what to say. Natalie didn't wait for a response.

"To heck with it."

She hadn't driven all the way out to Timbuktu, or spent money she could barely afford on fuel, just to turn around and go home. She pulled farther forward, but she hadn't angled her truck properly. Her power steering had gone out recently, which meant getting her vehicle any closer to the intercom would be like wrangling a hippopotamus next to a mailbox. She opened the truck's door, the hinges creaking in protest, and stepped out on the asphalt. She tried the obvious first, pressing zero on the keypad, and was surprised at the almost immediate "Hello."

"Colt?"

Silence. She didn't think he could possibly recognize her voice and so she said, "It's me, Natalie."

"I know who it is."

He knew? How? Was there a camera, too? She glanced at the sign hanging overhead and smiled, just in case. "Can I come in?"

She felt like an idiot. Maybe she should have listened to Jillian. Maybe she should have called ahead first, made an appointment.

She pressed the button again and spoke into the intercom. "Hello?"

The gates started to open, a beeping sound emerging from somewhere. Natalie was impressed by the high-tech-ness of it all.

Well, all righty then.

She went to shove a hank of hair out of her face, only to realize—yet again—that she had none, so settled instead for running her fingers through the short strands. At least he hadn't told her to leave. She was about to get back in her truck when she heard, "Veer right at the Y."

She didn't waste any time, gunning it so that her tires chirped on the blacktop, her struts and springs popping and moaning when the asphalt ended beyond the gate and turned into gravel. A glance in her rearview mirror revealed the gates already closing, which made her wonder if there were pressure plates. Somehow she hadn't figured Colt to be a big fan of new fangled devices. Clearly she'd been wrong.

The road led toward some low-lying hills. Grass and trees were the only things she could see as she got closer, her truck leaving a rooster tail of dust behind her. But like theater curtains, the hills seemed to part. Up ahead the road split into a Y, the branch on her right ending at a place she couldn't see. The road to her left, well, she couldn't see where that went, either, at least not at first. Soon buildings came into view. Big house at the end of the road with a massive oak tree in the front yard, barn to the right. Huge rose bushes lined the front, the kind that had been there forever, the home seeming to have been randomly plopped down in the middle of nowhere. Prairie grass stretched as far as the eye could see.

She'd taken her foot off the accelerator, slowing down so she could observe. Trucks and trailers were parked in front.

Crud.

He had company. Oh, well, she thought. He wouldn't have buzzed her through if he hadn't wanted her to intrude.

She turned her attention to her surroundings. The two-story homestead seemed old, but she would bet at one point it'd been considered a mansion in these parts. It was painted white, and was perfectly square but for a small portion that jutted out on the right side in a hexagonal shape. There were windows all around it and the cutest little gingerbread roofline. Along the lower left side of the home sat an old-fashioned porch, the kind with blooming potted plants hanging between fancy scalloped braces. It wrapped around the side and front edges of the home.

Colt had parked his trailer next to the porch, which seemed dumb considering it probably blocked his view of the rolling foothills and nearby mountains. Natalie's gaze moved to the barn to the right. Nothing fancy, just what appeared to be an old hayloft converted into a horse stable—she glimpsed stalls inside. By far the newest addition had to be the arena off behind the barn. State of the art by the looks of it, with a matching round pen outside. Both training areas had sand footing and high wooden rails that had been left natural in color so that they matched the big barn.

When she pulled up next to one of the four trucks

parked out front she couldn't help but admire their shiny exteriors. Her own truck was at least twenty years old and looked the part.

Feminine giggles.

They were the first thing to greet her—that and the sound of a bluebird warbling off in the distance. She didn't know why the laughter took her aback. She'd figured Colt wasn't the type to spend time with female company, had assumed the horses she saw saddled inside the trailer belonged to men.

No, he just didn't want to spend time with you.

Okay, fine. Back when she'd been her old self, she'd been a little miffed that he'd given her the cold shoulder at Zach and Mariah's wedding. She wasn't used to men doing that and, quite frankly, when she'd first met him she'd kicked herself for not agreeing to go on a date with him. He was a handsome cuss. Not that he'd asked, but Wes had offered to set them up at least a half-dozen times. She hadn't wanted a thing to do with a *cowboy* back then. Not her type. And then she'd met him and been instantly struck by that tingling in the pit of her belly, the only thought in her mind: *oh my*.

She rounded the open doorway of the barn and drew up short. Women. Five of them. All good looking. All cowgirls judging by the tight-fitting jeans and T-shirts. All standing in the middle of the barn, a row of stalls to their left and what must have been three tons of hay piled high to their right. The women turned to stare at her as though she was a poppy seed stuck in someone's teeth.

"Hey." She hated sounding so uncertain of herself because standing just beyond them was Colt in a black button-up and pressed jeans. "Sorry to drop in on you like this." She pointed over her shoulder. "But I was hoping we could talk."

He didn't seem angry that she'd tracked him down at his ranch. He didn't seem anything at all, although it was hard to gauge the emotions in his eyes beneath his cowboy hat. He stood just inside the barn, in front of the first stall.

"Natalie, meet the Galloping Girlz. Trick riders. They'll be performing with me out on the road."

Trick riders. Ah. They had the look of performers. Pretty. Skinny. Self-confident. She estimated most of them to be younger than she was, although one of them, a brunette, seemed about her age. Inside the barn it was dark, the only light coming from the massive front entrance, but when that brunette narrowed her gaze, her lashes following the lowered sweep of her eyes, it wasn't too dim for Natalie to spot the curiosity spilling from their blue depths.

"Samantha here is their leader."

"Hi." The woman charged toward Natalie and clasped her hand in her grip like a cowgirl wrangling a heifer. "Call me Sam." She pointed a thumb in Colt's direction. "Colt's the only one allowed to call me Samantha."

Natalie would have to be deaf not to hear the possessiveness in the woman's voice. She had long dark hair pulled back in a ponytail, the strands around her head held back by a crystal-studded headband that caught the light and sparkled in a way that matched the rhinestones on the front of her shirt. The woman was pretty, for all that she seemed to have the wrong idea about Natalie and Colt.

"We were actually just talking about you," Colt offered.

When Natalie caught Colt's gaze she still couldn't tell what ideas ran through his head. He didn't seem happy to see her. Then again, he didn't seem upset, either.

"Uh oh." She shot Samantha a smile meant to project: *Friendly! Nice! Not interested in Colt!* "I hope that's a good thing."

"Sam's been trying something new." Natalie watched to see if Colt reciprocated Sam's feelings, but the man was good at hiding his thoughts. "She wants to jump through a flaming hoop, but she's having trouble." Natalie couldn't be certain, but she thought that might be amusement she saw in Colt's eyes. "I told her she'd be lucky if she didn't set herself on fire."

"Colt." Sam made a big show of punching him in the shoulder before turning back to Natalie. "Colt tells me you used to be some big, famous jumping person."

Internationally famous. Ranked first in the world. Everyone had said 2016 would have been her year, the year she'd represent the United States in the games. And then the accident.

"I did okay."

There were times when disappointment and sorrow came out of nowhere and smacked her in the face. This was one of those moments, though she tried to hide it. When she met Colt's gaze, his amusement faded.

"We were hoping you could help." He gave her a small smile, one meant to tell her without words that he understood.

She took a deep breath, got hold of her emotions,

and pulled her shoulders back. "Well it's a good thing I showed up here then, isn't it?"

"So you'll do it?" Sam asked.

"Of course."

"Wait, wait." Colt held up his hands. "I told Sam she had to give you something in return."

Sam's whole face lit up with excitement. "I'm going to teach you to trick ride."

Chapter Four

He thought she'd be thrilled. Working with the Galloping Girlz would be an excellent way for Natalie to build upper body strength, not to mention recover her center of gravity.

Natalie didn't seem thrilled. She seemed terrified. "Oh, wow."

But the subtext of her words clearly indicated she'd rather jump out of an airplane—without a parachute.

"We can talk about it later." He motioned to the Galloping Girlz. "I think Sam would appreciate some help with Roger today.

"I would. He keeps stopping and I don't know why."

"Why don't you unload your horses?" Colt eyed the girls. "I can talk to Natalie about my idea alone."

"Sure," Sam said, corralling her teammates, but not before shooting Colt one last smile, a grin that slid off the edge of her face when her eyes fell on Natalie. Colt made a mental note to set the record straight with Sam even though he'd told her half a dozen times already—he wasn't interested in dating *anybody*.

"I didn't mean to interrupt your plans for the day," Natalie ventured.

For some reason Colt had a hard time meeting Natalie's eyes. Now that he thought about it, he'd had trouble with that since the moment he'd first met her. Something about her pretty blue gaze made him uncomfortable.

"No. It's okay. I should have called you before now anyway."

"But you weren't going to, were you?"

He prided himself on being honest in most situations, but he wouldn't be human if he didn't get a little hot under the collar thanks to the guilt her words evoked. "Tell you the truth, I wasn't. Well, I was. I was going to call to tell you to find someone else."

She seemed surprised by his frankness, her long lashes parting a bit before swooping down to shield those amazing blue eyes from his stare. "But now you want me to work with Sam. What changed your mind?"

"You showed up at my front gate." He shook his head. "And that tells me you're stubborn, and that you probably wouldn't take no for an answer."

"I wouldn't have."

"But you're scared."

That caught her off guard. "What makes you say that?"

"The look on your face when Sam volunteered to teach you trick riding."

"I told you my equilibrium is all messed up."

It wasn't just that. He could tell that she was holding something back. "Are you afraid of falling off?"

Her blue eyes suddenly grew two inches wide.

"You are, aren't you?"

She pulled her gaze away once again, as if sensing

he could read the thoughts in them. "Well, I should be a little cautious, don't you think? I mean, I'm basically learning how to ride all over again."

Cautious, yes. Terrified, no.

But he had some experience with how she felt. He'd taken a nasty tumble off a bronc once. Took him nearly a year to get back into the groove of things. And then even more recently, when he'd been caught in a fire fight near the border of Benghazi, it'd taken months before he could head out to patrol without getting the shakes. The thing with the military, though, was that you didn't have a choice. He might never have gotten over his fear if he'd been allowed to slink away.

"They say the best thing is to get back on the horse, and in my experience, that's proven to be true."

"I didn't fall off the last time I rode," she protested.

"No. Playboy took off with you. In some ways that can be worse."

She didn't deny it, but he could tell she still didn't want to try trick riding.

"Look, when I was younger I started riding broncs. I don't know if you know or not, but there's no steering a bucking horse. Took me a while to get used to having no control. It's going to take a while for you, too."

"But that's just it." She splayed her hands. "Bridleless reining is all about control."

He shook his head. "When it comes to horses, control is an illusion. They can always do what they want if they decide to. They're bigger, faster and, in some cases, smarter than a lot of humans. But all that doesn't matter because first you have to learn how to trust them or none of your goals will be possible." He crossed his arms in front of him. "Riding with the Galloping Girlz will be the best thing for you."

"What will I be doing?"

"That's up to Sam. She's the pro."

She didn't want to do it. Not at all.

"This is a deal breaker for me, Natalie. Either you let the girls help you out or I'm done."

He could see that she didn't take kindly to his ultimatum, but he was doing it for her own good. Just like in the military, sometimes it was better for people if they weren't given a choice. Tough love, so to speak.

Those eyes of hers had gone from big and uncertain to narrowed and annoyed. His words seemed to serve as a challenge. "Fine."

"You'll do it?"

"It seems I have no choice."

Good for her. He had to squelch the unexpected surge of admiration he felt. "Are you sure?"

"Of course I am."

He shook his head. "I don't know. I can see the fear in your eyes. It makes me wonder if you're ready. Maybe you should take some time off. Learn how to knit or something. When you're ready to get back on a horse you'll know."

"I'm not afraid to get back on a horse."

Tell it to the judge.

But he didn't say the words aloud. "Good," he said instead. "Because I think you should start working with Sam today."

"Today?" Her lips went slack.

"No time like the present."

He left her standing there because damned if he

didn't want to tell her everything would be okay. That he'd been in her shoes. That it would all work out. And even crazier, he had to fight the urge to pull her into his arms and reassure her with a hug.

I must be going soft in my old age.

IT'LL BE ALL RIGHT. *You'll be okay. Colt won't let you fall on your head.*

And die.

"You really don't need a helmet," Sam said, the bay gelding she held standing by her side patiently. "I promise not to let you fall on your head and die."

The words so closely echoed Natalie's thoughts that she almost let out a burst of laughter. Of course, it might sound a little hysterical right now, but at this point she really didn't care.

"Where I come from if you don't wear a helmet, you're considered insane." She saw Sam's eyes flash. "Not that I'm calling you insane, it's just a mind-set kind of thing."

Sam glanced at Colt, and Natalie could perfectly interpret the look she gave him. It was one of shared amusement. Only Colt didn't seem amused. He peered at them from his position alongside the rail of the arena. They stood in the sand, the other girls already on their horses and riding around. The first time she'd seen one of the pretty blondes stand on top of a saddle she'd felt physically nauseous.

There was no way they'd ask her to do that. Not yet, at least.

"Go on. Climb aboard."

It was at that moment that Natalie admitted to herself that Colt was right. She'd lost her nerve.

"I'd still feel better if I had something on my head." She pointed toward her hair. "I just had a traumatic brain injury."

Her chest felt tight. Anxiety. No denying it.

Sam had begun to study her closely, perhaps a little too closely. Did she know how near Natalie was to panic? "Colt, don't you have a helmet in the barn? I thought I saw one hanging there."

"I do." Without another word he turned to go get it.

It was a way to stall, the helmet issue, Natalie acknowledged inwardly. Well, not really. She truly didn't want to ride without the proper safety equipment, but the temporary delay gave her time to gather the reins of her nerve and analyze why she felt the way she did. Yes, she'd fallen off. Ironically, she'd been critically injured but the horse she'd been riding had been just fine, so she wasn't afraid of hurting another horse. Besides, she'd ridden Playboy recently and she hadn't been half as afraid as she was now.

"You don't have to do this, you know."

When Natalie looked up, Sam's eyes had lost their edge. She peered at her with something close to pity on her face. "We can do something else to get you back into shape, something that doesn't involve a horse."

Was her fear that obvious?

"No, no." Damn it. She could do this. She *would* do this. She turned toward the gelding next to her. "At least your horse is low to the ground. I won't have to look like a rock climber trying to scale Half Dome."

Humor. A defense mechanism. Before a big competition she'd always been the one to crack jokes. Laughter helped ground her. It reminded her that life shouldn't be taken too seriously. Everyone was going to die. One should enjoy the moment.

Just then one of the Galloping Girlz went by on her horse. The woman hung upside down off the side of her mount. Natalie gulped.

"I'm not doing that."

Sam followed her gaze and smiled. "Not yet."

Not ever.

"Here you go."

Natalie turned. Colt stood there with the helmet. An ugly white thing that resembled the top of a golf ball.

"Thanks."

When she met his gaze, she tried unsuccessfully to shield her thoughts from him.

You'll be all right.

The words were unspoken, but she heard them anyway. And suddenly she knew everything *would* be okay. He wouldn't let her get hurt. That wasn't his style. The man was a protector. A warrior. A good guy.

She tipped her chin up. "Let's do this."

She slipped on the helmet. It was a little too big, but it would do. Sam held the reins as she prepared to mount. She paused before getting on. Sam's patient gelding cocked an ear in her direction.

Nothing to be afraid of. The arena floor was soft. Even if she did fall off, chances were she wouldn't strike her head on the ground hard enough to jolt her brain. Thereby causing a seizure. One that might lead to permanent damage or even the end of her life.

"What's his name?" She grabbed the saddle horn. Although the horse was small by her standards—she was used to animals at least a foot taller than this one—it still felt like climbing a mountain.

"Roger."

"So this is the horse that refuses to jump?"

"It is."

She swung aboard. The way her heart pounded against her ribcage one would have thought she'd saddled a wild tiger. Good heavens, what was with her? She'd never been afraid of a horse a day in her life.

She caught Colt's gaze. He knew what a struggle it'd been for her to climb on, and the realization humiliated her. It shouldn't matter what he thought—she didn't even think he liked her—but for some reason it did.

"Too bad you can't take him over some fences for me." Sam met Natalie's gaze. "Colt told me you were in a horse wreck. What happened?"

"I don't know." Natalie fingered a strand of Roger's black mane. "I was told my horse slipped before a jump, but I don't remember anything."

"Wow. Was the horse okay?"

"He was fine. Me? Not so much." It still freaked her out that she couldn't recall the accident. No matter how hard she tried—it just wasn't there. "They have it on video, but the angle's all wrong. He might have chipped a bit, might have slipped, might have spooked at something. All I know is he took off wrong and landed in the middle of a five foot fence."

"Five feet?"

Talking was good. Talking meant she didn't have to move. When she put a horse into motion she began to suffer dizzy spells. It wasn't so bad if she walked, but anything faster and she might as well be riding the Tilt-O-Whirl at the fair.

"Fortunately it wasn't during a jump-off or it might have been higher."

"Why don't you take Roger out to the rail?" Sam suggested.

They both glanced toward Colt and Natalie could tell nothing escaped his notice. He knew she was stalling for time. Could he see the way her hands shook? Had he spotted her pulse beating at her neck? The way her hands clenched and unclenched on the reins? She would swear her heart could be heard outside her body.

"Come on." She clucked, but the moment the horse took a step forward she wanted to throw up, and not just because of the way moving made her feel. There was the fear she battled back. The sickness at realizing she wasn't the same as before and might never be. The shame of knowing she hadn't been honest with Colt and the admission that she owed him the truth.

"Whoa."

The horse obeyed instantly, his head lifting a notch as she pulled back on the reins.

"What's the matter?" Colt asked from the rail.

She'd had a traumatic brain injury, damn it. She'd damaged her inner ear.

"I just need a moment."

"Time out."

Natalie's head snapped up, causing her to clutch mane. "I don't need a time out. I just need a moment to adjust to the sudden change in elevation."

Too late. Colt walked toward her. He eyed Sam. "Give us a second, would you, Sam?"

The woman nodded, shooting Natalie a look of encouragement before taking Colt's place on the rail.

"When you said you had balancing issues, exactly what did you mean?" He asked.

"I told you, I can't ride English anymore. Lifting my body up and down makes me so dizzy I nearly came off the first time I rode."

"You also said you could ride Western."

"And I can." She held Colt's gaze, a part of her wanting to tell him the truth, the whole truth, but if she did that, she knew she'd lose her last best chance of ever riding again. "Like I said, I just need a moment."

"You haven't even broken a walk and you're already clutching mane."

She immediately released the strands of black horse hair. "All better." She lifted her hands. "See?"

He didn't look as if he believed her, his golden eyes nearly as dark as the black felt of his cowboy hat. "Exactly what happened when you rode Playboy without a bridle?"

"What do you mean?"

"I want to know the details. Were you walking? Trotting? Galloping?"

She didn't want to answer because by doing so she would reveal more than she wanted him to know. "I was just walking."

He crossed his arms, tipping back to stare up at her in a way that had her wanting to break the connection of their gaze. "And had you ever trotted since your accident?"

And there it was. The question she'd feared. "No."

He tipped back farther. "Cantered?"

She took a deep breath. "No."

"So all you've done since your wreck is walk?"

Another deep breath. "Yes."

"And you decided on that day to practice walking without a bridle?"

"You make it sound like I'm crazy."

"What happened when you dropped the bit?"

"At first, nothing."

"And then?"

One of the girls in the arena galloped by again, this one hanging off the back of her mount so that her head rested near her horse's tail. *Dear Lord.* Never mind how painful it must be to have the cantle of the saddle digging into your—

"Natalie?"

"Once he realized he had no bridle Playboy started to trot."

"Were you able to hang on?"

"At first." Her fingers found mane again and she dug her hands into the silky strands. "But then he started to canter, and the up-and-down motion, well, let's just say it made things more difficult."

"Exactly *how* difficult."

"I nearly blacked out."

"Son of a—" If he'd been the demonstrative type she had a feeling he would have thrown his hat at her.

"But I hung on." Somehow she had, although to this day she didn't know how. She couldn't recall Jillian running into the arena, or her friend stepping in front of Playboy and somehow managing to get him stopped. She half-suspected she'd had her eyes closed the whole time. All she knew was that one moment the horse had been running full-tilt and the next she was being helped down to the ground.

"I vomited afterward."

If Colt had been a character in a sitcom he would have stormed off set. Instead he just stood there, mouth partly open, and though she sat above him by a good two feet, she somehow felt about three feet smaller.

"Why is it every time I talk to you I discover something new? Something I'm not happy to discover. Something that smacks of dishonesty?"

Because she had been dishonest. About one thing at least.

"Because if I told you the whole story, you'd never have agreed to help me, would you?"

She had him there. The brim of his cowboy hat lowered so that she couldn't see his face. He appeared to be watching one of the Galloping Girlz, this one on a sorrel. Natalie watched, too, because the woman had hooked her foot into a loop near the skirt of the saddle. She anticipated what would happen next and sure enough, the pretty blonde stood up, hooking her other foot through a matching loop on the other side. She stood. No reins. No control. No fear. It took Natalie's breath away because it was both awe-inspiring and death defying, the woman's blond ponytail streaming out behind her.

"I won't be doing that anytime soon."

Colt's gaze shot to her own. She saw a flicker of amusement, but only for a moment.

"Probably not."

His shoulders lifted and then relaxed, as if he'd

taken a deep breath, one filled with resignation. Her own breathing slowed.

"All right, look, we're going to work on some simple balancing techniques today. I'm going to put you out on a lunge line, have you close your eyes, keep you focused on staying aboard, not what your head is telling you might happen."

She used to do that to the kids she taught. The five-year-olds.

Now, now. You have to start somewhere.

"And tomorrow?"

"More balancing exercises."

She nodded. "Whatever we have to do."

"But I can't work with you every day. Maybe Sam can, but I have performances most weekends."

"I know."

"But I'll do what I can. And we can talk to Sam and see if she can help you when I'm not around."

Natalie wanted to cry, except she couldn't because if she did she'd seem like a sissy and she had a feeling Colt didn't deal well with sissies.

"You're going to feel like a kid learning to ride all over again, and when you're not working with Sam or me, I think you should sign up for a rehabilitation program, one that specializes in hippotherapy."

Hippotherapy. Translation: equine therapy. She'd resisted doing that, hadn't thought it was necessary. Clearly, she'd been kidding herself. She trusted Colt, and if he said she needed outside help, well maybe it was time to put her pride aside.

"In the meantime bring Playboy over here and I'll start working with him for you. It'll be easier for me to prep him for reining competitions."

Her eyes burned. She realized that she was fighting back sudden tears. She had to blink a few times. "Thanks, Colt."

"Don't thank me yet." He slapped Roger's neck. "Let's see how you do today before you start getting excited."

Chapter Five

He'd tortured her for an hour.

Natalie had been a saint through it all. Colt had known his ultimatum would leave her with little choice but to do as he asked, and truthfully, he'd half-hoped she'd say no so he'd be off the hook with very little guilt. She'd agreed, though, and then worked hard, despite having to stop from time to time to settle her stomach. Afterward, she'd spent a good hour working with Sam and Roger over a few pieces of wood. She called it ground work, but it wasn't the kind he was used to. Natalie had said that using the wooden obstacles was the first step to teaching Roger how to jump.

"You look lost in thought."

Colt glanced up at his sister, Claire. They were sitting in her kitchen, him about to embark on babysitting duties, her heading off to town to run errands. Claire lived on the property, in what had been called the cowboy bunkhouse back when their dad had run a few hundred head of cattle. She'd converted the place into a home, and the siblings now lived a good mile away from each other, Colt at one end of the two-hundred-acre parcel and Claire at the other. He'd always liked the spot where she lived—at the base of a small hill, surrounded by a grove of oak trees with a year-round creek within walking distance—better than the site where his grandfather had built the main homestead, out in the middle of nowhere so he could keep an eye on things, or so Colt had been told.

"I was thinking about that woman I'm helping," he answered.

"Natalie, right?" Claire swept her long, black hair over one shoulder, the strands twisting in a way that somehow made it look thicker. "Wes and Jillian's friend."

He fingered the tab top of a soda can, twanging it as he recalled his first lesson with Natalie. "She popped in on me today."

Wide, sweeping black brows lifted. "Oh, yeah?"

Adam, Colt's five-year-old nephew, sat in the small living area near the front of the cozy but comfortable open-concept house. He was busy snapping together some kind of Lego war craft, probably from the latest superhero movie, *Hawkman*. The boy loved comic books. When Adam glanced up, Colt found himself smiling, once again surprised at how much he looked like Claire. That was a good thing. Not just because she was good-looking, but because he couldn't imagine Claire having to stare at Marcus's face day in and day out.

"We ended up tormenting her in the arena."

Claire took a pull from her own soda, clearly not in any hurry to set off on her trip to town.

"*We* being you and your new harem," she said, a teasing glint coming into her bright green eyes.

"Claire!"

Her smile could light up a room and right then, it did. "What? You know it's true. Sam has had the hots for you since you came back from the Middle East."

"Not interested."

"Why not? She's pretty, that's for sure."

"You know why." He peered at Claire in a way she couldn't fail to recognize.

Her smile faded. "You're still convinced you're damaged goods."

"It's proven to be a little more than a theory by now." But he didn't like to think about his failed romances, nor the scars that fire fight near Benghazi had left behind. "Anyway, we worked Natalie pretty hard."

He could tell Claire wanted to continue the conversation about his love life, but she wisely changed her mind. "What do you mean? I thought you were helping her with her horse?"

He really wished his soda was a beer. He could have used a long swig of something stronger right then. "Turns out she needs as much work as her horse."

"I thought she was some kind of famous English rider."

"She was. She had an accident." He tapped his head. "It's messed up her balance pretty good."

As he thought back to earlier in the day, and how hard Natalie had fought not only to stay atop Roger, but to keep herself from getting sick, something damn near like admiration made one side of his mouth curl.

"You like her."

His head jerked upward. "Excuse me?"

"This woman. You like her. I saw the way you just smiled."

"I didn't smile." He leaned back in his chair and peered out the window by the kitchen table where they sat. "It was a smirk."

"I can tell the difference between a smirk and a smile."

He shook his head. "Don't be confusing admiration with interest."

"Why not? They're two sides of the same coin."

"It's not like that." Colt shot his sister a glare.

"Is she pretty?"

Instantly, Natalie's jewel-like eyes came to mind. They were blue-tinted stained glass windows to her soul. Not just pretty. Stunning.

"She is, isn't she?" Claire wriggled in her chair. "And you—" she made quotes with her fingers "—admire her. This ought to be interesting."

Colt ignored her. "Do me a favor. Go on and get out of here. I'd like to spend some quality time with my nephew, if you don't mind."

It was her turn to smirk, but Claire was smart. She knew when to push an issue and when to pull back. So she stood and reached behind her, pulling the cowhide straps of her brown purse over her shoulder.

"Fine." She leaned down and kissed the top of his head, the gesture so reminiscent of when they had been kids, it brought a lump to Colt's throat. "I won't be gone long. I just need to pick up some dog food from the feed store and run by Adam's doctor's office to sign some insurance papers. I shouldn't be gone more than an hour."

He lifted a hand in acknowledgment. His nephew

hadn't been feeling well lately. Some kind of persistent flu, but Claire had told him Adam had been bouncing off the walls earlier so he planned to take the boy back to his own place, put him up on one of the horses, and help him burn off some energy.

"But for the record." Claire paused with her hand on the old-fashioned knob. "I don't think you're as damaged as you think. I think you're one of the most amazing men I know. Well, aside from Chance." Her smile turned sad for a moment because she missed their little brother, a man who'd dedicated his life to the military in a way Colt might have, too, if he hadn't been pressured to come home when their dad had gotten sick. "But that goes without saying. Anyway, my point is that someday some woman is going to challenge you to be the man I've always known you could be. I just hope I'll still be living here so I can be around to see it."

COLT HAD TOLD HER to bring Playboy over the next day and Natalie wasted no time in taking him up on the offer. These days she had to borrow a trailer—yet another thing she'd had to sell—from a friend. Playboy didn't seem to mind.

Colt had given her the gate code so she drove right in unannounced. She worried Colt would be out, but it turned out she'd feared needlessly. His pretty truck with all its fancy logos sat right where it'd been parked yesterday, but today there was another truck next to it. She wondered if he had company. A girlfriend perhaps? And why did that give her pause? Whether he dated someone such as Sam or this month's cover girl, it didn't matter. At least there weren't a million different vehicles out front. Ergo, she wouldn't be goaded into riding today. She couldn't imagine getting on a horse again so soon. Yesterday had been bad enough. All they'd done was walk, but even that had been difficult. It was her peripheral vision that messed her up—they'd figured out that if she closed her eyes, she didn't get as dizzy. It'd been something of a breakthrough and she had Colt to thank for figuring it out.

She pulled up in front of the barn. A horse inside neighed, and Playboy answered the call. It'd dawned overcast and cold in the morning, but the clouds had burned off leaving behind a glorious day. In the distance behind Colt's house, the grazing cows lifted their heads, eyes clearly peering in her direction. She turned her attention back to Playboy.

"You ready to learn how to be a trick horse?" She paused near the side of the trailer. The horizontal slats afforded her a perfect view of her animal in his rope halter. He didn't pay much attention to her; too busy looking around, ears pricking forward, then back, then forward again.

"Don't be nervous." She climbed up on the side of the wheel well, reached through the slats and rested a palm on Playboy's dark neck. "Colt's about as nice as they come."

To animals.

He'd been a harsh taskmaster yesterday. When she'd gotten one of her dizzy spells, he hadn't let her stop. He'd insisted she keep going. Told her to close her eyes and hang on, and if she started to fall he'd catch her. She hadn't fallen. Truth be told, it wasn't just the fear of hitting the ground that had kept her on board. It was pride. She'd be damned if she'd fall off in front of Colt and the Galloping Girlz.

She glanced toward the house, fully expecting to see Colt coming toward her. Surely he'd heard her pull up. The cobblestone path leading up to his front door stood empty. *Guess he didn't hear me arrive*, she thought, setting off in the direction of his home.

She heard the woman's voice before she saw her through the picture-frame window set beneath the home's front porch overhang. A dark-haired woman. Sam? Had she spent the night? Something curdled in Natalie's stomach. Had they talked about her after she'd left? Did they think her pathetic?

Stop it.

She took a deep breath. She might be broken, but she wasn't beaten, and she wasn't ashamed of her disability.

She found herself in front of a door the color of leather with four squares of beveled glass set into its center. All she could see through the panes were light and dark shadows. She lifted the horseshoe-shaped brass knocker and let it swing.

"Just a minute," Colt called from inside.

Goodness, she hoped they weren't half undressed. That would be embarrassing. No sooner had she had the thought than she spotted a dark shape approaching through the glass. The door swung wide and a harried looking Colt appeared before her.

"Sorry." He ran a hand through his thick black hair. "Bad time." He peered toward the stable area. "If you just want to put Playboy in the first stall on the left, I've already cleared a space for him."

"Actually—" A woman as beautiful as a Bond girl

appeared behind Colt. She had clearly been crying. "I think I'll be heading home." She held the hand of a little boy, one with dark hair and dark green eyes like his mother. The woman shot Natalie a small, moisture-filled smile, before turning to Colt. "I had things to do today, and I just thought…"

The woman's words trailed off as tears reappeared on her lashes. She looked steadily at Colt, multiple emotions floating through her eyes, emotions that Natalie couldn't put a name to. No. That wasn't precisely true. She recognized pain. Sadness. Fear.

What was going on?

"Claire, no. You should stay here. Let's talk some more."

"Mommy, I'm tired."

They both looked at the little boy. Natalie's whole body tensed when she spotted the same sort of emotions in Colt's eyes.

"Of course you are, baby," the woman said, and she shot Colt such a look of helplessness that Natalie found herself stepping back.

"I'll go put Playboy away."

Colt stared at Natalie and it was the first time she had seen him looking so vulnerable. She gave him a small smile, the reaction instinctive, the urge to say something comforting nearly overwhelming. She had a feeling she'd interrupted something important. Something life-changing. Whatever it was, she knew she should leave and give them some space.

It was almost a relief when they closed themselves back inside. She paused at the top of the steps, hearing the quiet murmur of voices resuming, and glanced up at the sky. She remembered when she'd woken up in the hospital, unable to move, helpless, and how she'd looked out her hospital window and thought how odd it seemed that the sun still rose in the east and set in the west. People still went to work every morning. Life went on, but her life, her small slice of the world, had been changed irrevocably in the blink of an eye. At the very least there should have been a clap of thunder.

She would leave, she thought, unloading Playboy. Come back later when whatever calamity had beset Colt's life had had time to sink in. But as she unclipped the lead, tapping Playboy on the withers to send him inside his new stall, she knew that might be a while. When she turned to leave, she had a moment of dizziness, her hands instinctively reaching for the stall door she'd been about to swing closed.

"Careful."

And suddenly he was there, supporting her, making sure she didn't topple over, and she was looking into his eyes and thinking it wasn't fair that there was so much sadness in the world.

"I'm okay." She'd clutched Colt's forearms, and the material of his denim shirt felt coarse beneath her fingers, his muscles hard. When she met his gaze, she heard herself ask, "Are you?"

She hadn't meant to pry. Truly she hadn't. The words felt as if they'd been pulled from her by something bigger than she was, something that recognized the look in his eyes as one she knew. Grief.

"I'm fine."

He pushed away, ostensibly to peer at Playboy, his face in profile. The only light in the barn came from the massive front entrance. She saw Colt's jaw tick, the muscle flexing in a way that told her he was clenching his teeth as firmly as he was his hands.

"Colt, I'm sorry."

He shook his head. His hand relaxed. He threw his shoulders back as if facing off with an inner demon only he could see.

"It's nothing."

There was one thing she'd learned from her accident and that was to live in the moment. Perhaps that was why she reached for his hand, why she slipped her fingers into his. She didn't know him all that well, but she recognized a human in pain.

Outside, a truck started. He jerked his hand from hers and turned toward the entryway. A second later the woman drove by. The little boy in the front seat waved.

"Adam," she heard Colt mutter. "Son of a bitch."

She took a step back, so much pain, so much fear, so much sadness in his words it was like a physical slap.

"Goddamn *son* of a *bitch.*"

He waved at the disappearing truck until he couldn't see it anymore. Then he turned back toward the barn. Natalie had no idea what he was about to do until he did it, picking up a bucket and pitching it at the hay pile hard enough that it clattered and fell to the ground, startling the horses in the barn.

"Colt."

It sounded as if the bucket had broken. He didn't seem to care, just moved to the pile, turned his back to her and stood there. She heard a horse snort, then nothing. Silence descended.

That was when she heard it, his voice so low she would have missed it if it hadn't been so quiet outside.

"My nephew has cancer."

Chapter Six

"Oh, dear Lord."

Colt heard Natalie's words, but told himself not to say more. It wasn't any of her business. He could handle his own problems, like he always had.

Adam had cancer.

He wasn't certain he could handle that.

"How bad?" she asked.

He shouldn't have said anything, damn it, didn't want to talk about it. "Bad enough that he has to go in for a battery of tests this week." Colt's breaths came faster and faster. "Goddamn it. He's just a kid. He should be playing with his *Hawkman* action figure, not dealing with a deadly disease."

"I'm sorry."

How could it be possible? How could his curious, rambunctious *five-year-old nephew* have cancer? Cancer was for old people. For people who smoked or who tanned too much. It wasn't for little children.

"What kind?"

He rounded on her. "They don't know yet. Some kind of blood something."

Natalie had taken a small step back, blue eyes wide, and it occurred to him that she'd been through her own kind of personal hell and didn't deserve his anger. That's what he was—angry. No. Enraged. His poor sister had been through enough already what with the death of Marcus. She'd spent enough time in hospitals. She didn't deserve this. Adam didn't deserve this. None of them did.

Colt hadn't even realized he'd closed his eyes until he felt Natalie's hand on his arm again. He told himself to pull away, but when he opened his eyes to do exactly that, something in her gaze caught him.

"What can I do to help?" she offered.

He took a deep breath, tried to calm his emotions. "Saddle up your horse so I can ride him."

Work. Work was the best thing for him. He had a rodeo this weekend and he'd been planning on heading out early. Now that wasn't possible. He wanted to be around for Adam's tests. But he could work here at home. He could keep himself busy, keep himself from thinking dark and horrible thoughts.

Natalie did as he asked without question. He had no idea how she'd known which saddle to use. He had several of them, but she'd picked his work saddle, although he didn't recognize the bridle. Must have been hers. When she'd finished she stepped back.

"He's pretty light in the bridle."

He didn't comment. His hands shook as he reached for the reins.

Adam had cancer.

He wanted to wrench the reins from her hands. To jump aboard and gallop off into the distance. To forget what he knew with the help of a long ride. Alas, the words in his head and the dark, terrible thoughts they roused weren't going anywhere.

"Does he neck rein?" Colt put a foot in the stirrup.

Natalie seemed offended. "Of course. I'm not a complete idiot."

No. She'd been a sweetheart, he thought, swinging up onto the dark bay gelding. She'd put up with his fury without flinching. Well, maybe she'd flinched a little. But yesterday… She'd been a trooper, then, too.

When he settled into the saddle his world tipped back to normal, or at least a little more normal than before. They would get through this, just as they'd gotten through Marcus's illness.

Marcus had died.

Adam would not. Colt would be damned before he watched his nephew lose the upcoming battle, and a battle it would be.

"Thank you." He patted Playboy.

A blond brow lifted. "For what?"

He took a moment to gather his thoughts, played with the tips of the reins, then dropped them so they hung down the horse's neck.

"For doing what I asked and not asking a million questions."

"You need space." She shrugged. "I know how that feels."

He knew she did. Wes had told him she'd hit rock bottom. Lost it all—her business, her show horses. Hell, even the place where she'd lived. The owner of the farm she used to lease had given her the boot when he realized she wouldn't be making him any money. From what Colt understood she now lived in a single bedroom apartment—a far cry from the lavish lifestyle she'd once lead in the prestigious show-jumping world. Yet there she stood, her pretty face smiling gently up at him. Not the least bit bitter, just determined. Yesterday had proven that.

"I need to ride, too," he admitted. "Maybe then the world will feel a little more familiar."

"It will," she said. "For a little while, at least."

He stared down at her, suddenly unable to move. She understood. Perhaps better than any other person in the world. The woman staring up at him had faced her own battle and come through on the other side. He would, too.

"Then let me ride."

COLT RODE PLAYBOY as though he'd been riding him his entire life, and the sight made Natalie want to cry. He got that horse to do things she could only dream about. When Colt stopped in the center of the ring and had Playboy spin in place Natalie held her breath, not just because the picture—mane flying, tail swishing, hooves dancing—was one that took her breath away, but because it struck her that she might never get to do that on her horse. Right now it was all she could do to stay on board at a walk.

Colt stopped spinning. Natalie's world kept tilting. Who was she trying to kid? There was no way in hell she could stick on for a spin like that.

"He's a good little horse." Colt called from the center of the arena, Playboy's nostrils flaring from his recent workout. "Gonna make a nice reiner."

For someone else. Not her. Not if she didn't start getting this vertigo under control. She almost laughed. Vertigo, hell, it wasn't just that. She'd been terrified yesterday. Terrified of just *riding*.

"Good, 'cause I've been wondering if I shouldn't sell him."

Colt looked up and she realized she'd caught him in the middle of thinking about his nephew. He had the air of a man who'd just watched a bomb explode. Who could blame him? That cute little boy and that beautiful woman who must be Colt's sister. What a terrible thing.

"Did you just say you might sell him?" He clucked Playboy forward, stopping him by the rail and climbing off of him. He walked the horse over to Natalie.

Hearing him say the words back to her made her realize the idea might not be crazy. She should be grateful for what she had. The use of her legs and a brain. That brain told her it was a stupid idea to pursue her dream of reining competitions.

"Colt, you and I both know I'm tackling the impossible here. You saw me yesterday."

At least she'd succeeded in turning his mind away from his nephew, if only for a little while. Colt might not seem happy right now, but she suspected that had to do with her declaration more than anything else.

"What I saw was a woman nearly crippled by fear."

"I know." She prided herself on being honest, even if the truth hurt. "But that's exactly my point. I'm in no condition to ride. Not now."

Maybe not ever.

"I just think maybe I need to slow down a little. Get my equilibrium problem sorted out without a horse being involved."

"The only way you're going to do that is by pushing yourself. Horse or no horse."

"I know."

"Although I think riding is the way to go." He nodded to emphasize his words. "I did some research last night on the internet. There's documented proof on how riding can help complications like yours. Something about reprogramming the brain. They say it's like any muscle. It requires work to get it back into shape."

She knew that. She'd not only read the same information, she'd been told by her neurologist. Only he'd said the words in a too-bad-you-can't-ride-anymore kind of way. She had decided to heed Colt's advice, though, and had signed up for a hippotherapy session. She started next week.

"I've read mountain biking can help, too," she ventured.

"To hell with tires. You've got a perfectly good horse right here. In fact, you should ride him right now."

Her heart began to beat like the thumping of a teenager's car with its stereo cranked. If someone had told her a year ago that she'd be terrified to get up on her own horse she'd have laughed them out of the room. Only now did she admit the bitter truth. That runaway ride on Playboy had scared her. Badly.

"Go on," Colt urged.

As if sensing Natalie's fear, Playboy turned to look back at her, his big brown eyes seeming to say, "It's all right."

It wasn't all right. She'd faced off with some of the best riders in the world over obstacles that would have given Superman pause, but her courage had crumbled to dust. Yesterday had done her in. She'd had nightmares about coming off again, horrible dreams where she'd seen the ground rushing up to meet her. She'd woken up with a headache that had made her want to vomit.

"You look a little green around the gills."

Her mouth was so dry she had to swallow before she could speak. "I am." She turned to face Colt. "Look at my hands." She held them flat, but they shook so badly she might have had another type of neurological disorder. "I'm absolutely terrified."

He held her gaze. Before she knew it he stood in front of her, right in front of her, and for the first time it occurred to her that he was quite a bit taller than she was, and wider, and despite the fact that there were times she despised him, in that moment all she wanted to do was collapse against his chest and cry like a baby. *What a boob. He* was the one who had something to cry about, not her.

"I know how you feel," he offered.

She latched onto the words like a lifeline. "Do you?"

He nodded. "Once, when I was younger, my dad put me up on his old ranch horse. Horse's name was Buddy and I swear to this day some old cowboy gave him that name as a joke. That horse was nobody's friend. My dad knew it. Just as he knew I had no business riding it. I couldn't have been more than six or seven, and that horse was near sixteen hands, but my dad threw me up and told me to hang on."

She could see a play of emotions cross Colt's face, most of which she couldn't name. The sight of him standing above her, so close, eyes flickering like an old picture show, fascinated her.

"Then my old man slapped that horse on the rear so hard it startled the chickens that used to roost in the barn there. Buddy took off for the hills." He pointed over his shoulder, all the while shaking his head. "I remember hanging on to that saddle horn so tight my fingers started to ache after the first mile, and that piece of you-know-what horse wasn't even close to slowing down. He must have run on for another half a mile before I saw it."

His eyes flashed again, dark lashes lowering, mouth firming. "Fence up ahead. I might have been a kid, but I knew that meant bad news. Barbed wire. If the horse didn't see it he'd run right into it, probably flipping over on me like I'd seen in the movies. If he saw it he might jump it or he might turn suddenly and pitch me off." He paused for a moment and Natalie watched, hardly breathing, as she waited for him to finish his tale.

"Buddy never slowed. When we were about twenty feet away I tried to clutch the saddle horn tighter. I think I was convinced I could keep myself on if I held the damn thing tight enough. I was wrong. Buddy didn't run through it or jump it or turn. He stopped. Hard. I didn't stand a chance. He launched me over his neck." He mimicked the motion with his hand, slapping his hand in his palm. "I flew so far I remember watching the ground whiz past me and thinking *this is going to hurt.* And it did. I hit—hard. Couldn't breathe. Had the wind knocked out of me. I was sure I'd broke my back."

She nodded in commiseration. "I've been launched like that before."

"Then you know what it's like, how much it hurts, and how there's that moment when you wonder, is this it? Will I be able to walk again?"

Yup. She knew that feeling. All too well, but she didn't feel the need to point that out to Colt.

"I just lay there for a long while, convinced my dad would ride up and carry me back to the ranch, but that didn't happen."

His eyes blazed. His jaw ticked. Clearly, the memory stirred up feelings that still affected him deeply.

"After a while I realized my dad wasn't coming. When I stood I nearly fell back down. I'd hurt my ankle pretty bad. I could feel it swelling inside my boot, but I was on my own, which meant either walking back to the ranch or climbing on top of that cantankerous piece of crap of a horse. Tell you the truth, that scared me more than anything else. What if he took off again? But I took one step and knew there was no way in hell I could walk all the way back."

"I take it Buddy didn't run off."

"Oh, no. He was right where he'd stopped, standing in the same place, by the fence. I swear he was watching me and laughing." He shook his head. "I still don't know how I did it. That barbed wire was old and the strands were close together but I somehow managed to slip through it without slicing myself to shreds. Buddy never moved as I tugged myself back on board, and when I picked up the reins, he behaved like a perfect gentleman. I sometimes wonder if he knew I was hurt. The only time he acted up was when we got close to home. He thought about making a run for it, but I was so mad at that damn horse that I jerked him around and made him behave."

"Where was your dad?"

"Gone."

She didn't quite understand. "You mean out looking for you?"

There it was again. The look. "Nope. Down to the local bar, gone."

He had to be joking. Trouble was, he didn't laugh. "Wasn't he worried about you?"

He looked away for a moment. "I doubt he even noticed I'd been missing."

She had a hard time believing that was true, yet he looked so serious. He didn't appear to want to talk about it, though.

"But that's not the point of my tale. The point is that sometimes we have to face our fears in order to overcome them."

He wasn't telling her anything she didn't already know. She'd given herself the same lecture when she'd climbed aboard Playboy after he'd run away with her. All she'd done was walk, but she'd told herself it was sufficient. Now she knew it hadn't been nearly enough. She should have done her regular training routine, ridden for at least a half-hour. Instead she'd used her vertigo as an excuse to call it a day. She'd used the same excuse for weeks.

"I sometimes think if my dad hadn't abandoned me, if he'd actually been there to scoop me up and tell me everything would be all right, I might never have ridden again. The experience was that terrifying."

"I know how that feels."

She couldn't look away from him, felt something inside her stir as she stared into his eyes, something that made her suddenly as fearful of him as she was of her horse.

Afraid of riding. Sad.

No, a little voice inside her said. *Afraid of dying.*

She had to look away from Colt. She sensed more than saw him move, couldn't believe it when she felt his hand touch her chin, gently lifting it so that she looked into his eyes, now a light brown. She had a feeling he didn't touch people very often. Animals, yes, but his fellow human beings, no.

"Life is short." The sun in his eyes disappeared. "Don't let fear get in the way of living."

Chapter Seven

He should heed his own advice.

Colt could barely breathe for the crippling fear that had overtaken him since his sister's devastating news. It was all he could do to stand there outside the arena and focus on Natalie when what he wanted to do was go inside, sit down, cover his face with his hands and cry. Poor Adam. The pain he'd go through while they tried to kill the damn piece of crap that was cancer...

"Colt?"

He refocused. Natalie stood in front of him and he realized he was holding his hand against her cheek. Suddenly, his thoughts spun in another direction. Briefly, but undeniably. Her short hair accentuated her heart-shaped face. Blue eyes that might have gotten lost beneath a mass of blond hair seemed huge. Those eyes were filled with sadness and longing and fear, emotions that made the pit of his stomach ache with sympathy and made him want to use his other hand to draw her nearer.

"Don't quit on me, Natalie."

Two weeks ago he would have seized the excuse to get out of helping her with her horse. Today he clung to the task like a man would a life raft.

"Okay." She licked her lips. "I won't."

He told himself to move away. To step back. He didn't. Only when Playboy began to move—the horse clearly impatient with standing around—did they break apart, Natalie to tug back on the reins, Colt to turn away.

Damn. What the hell had that been?

"Whoa, Playboy," he directed.

That's what he told himself, too. Whoa. He didn't need the distraction of Natalie's blue eyes. Not now. Not ever. He'd sworn off women and all the problems they entailed. His life was complicated enough as it was.

"I'll hold Playboy's reins if that will make you feel better."

"More pony rides?" She flicked her chin up—a habit of hers, he realized. "No thanks. I think it's time I rode on my own."

"Are you sure?"

She positioned herself by Playboy's stirrup and turned to face him. "If I don't do this now, I don't think I ever will."

Colt thought the same thing. "Just use your voice. That's why I gave you those exercises on the ground. He'll listen. I promise."

She was in profile to him, and he could see the determination on her face. As if doing a mental countdown in her head—three, two, one—she stared up at the seat of the saddle until, taking a deep breath, she hefted herself on board, her hands immediately clutching the horse.

"Good girl."

Natalie gripped the horn. Her shoulders were

hunched over. Her eyes were closed. Such a far cry from the rider she used to be that he couldn't speak for the surge of sympathy that filled him.

"I can do this," he heard her mutter. "I've ridden in international competition."

She would never ride at that level again. He had no doubt she'd regain some of her ability, but he'd read last night that equilibrium problems were nearly impossible to overcome entirely. She would always have issues with movement and changes in altitude. Jumping was out.

"Okay, I'm going to lead you around. Keep your eyes closed."

She nodded, still clutching the horn. He moved to Playboy's head and clucked. The horse immediately began to move with him and he glanced up at Natalie to ensure she was all right. One step and then two, three and then four. He'd be lying if he didn't admit his own anxiety on her behalf. As they walked, her shoulders began to relax. He turned left and Playboy followed. Colt saw her grasp the horn a little tighter when she sensed the change in direction, but she no longer sat like a kid on her first horse. She began to look more like an experienced rider. Back straight, elbows, legs and heels all in line. Her head came up and he knew she searched the darkness behind her eyes for her balance.

"Hang on," Colt advised.

Natalie's eyes popped open. "Why?"

"Just close your eyes and hang on."

"You're not going to trot, are you?"

"Don't worry about what I'm going to do, just focus on keeping your balance."

"Colt—"

He urged Playboy to trot.

"Colt, no—"

He ignored her. Playboy, good horse that he was, meekly followed alongside him, picking up the pace and moving into a trot. He thought he heard Natalie yelp and checked to ensure she was still all right, pleased to see that she was still holding on and that her eyes were closed once again.

"I'll stop if you start to fall."

But she didn't fall. She didn't even slip off to the side. She went back to riding like a novice, but only for the first half-circle they trotted. By the time they'd completed one big loop she'd begun to relax. More than that, she began to smile.

"Do you think you can open your eyes?"

The smile faded. "I'd rather not."

"I think you should."

"What if I get dizzy again?"

"I'll catch you."

He could tell she didn't want to. Jogging alongside her, he could only catch quick glimpses of her face, but her fear and insecurity seemed to ooze from every pore.

Her eyes opened.

He caught the moment, took care to ensure he kept his eyes on her, no easy feat while guiding a horse. He thought she might close them quickly, but she didn't. Instead she stared straight ahead, such an intense look of concentration on her face he couldn't help but admire her fortitude.

He hoped to God he could face Adam's coming battle as bravely.

The thought took the steam out of him. He pulled Playboy up. Natalie's gaze swung toward him, the smile on her face growing in size to the point that his plummeting spirits lifted momentarily.

"I did it."

He wouldn't have been human if he didn't return her smile. "You did."

"And I didn't barf all over you."

"That's definitely a good thing."

And suddenly she was laughing and patting Playboy's neck and looking so proud of herself that Colt knew he'd made the right decision in pushing her.

HE BAILED ON their next training session, not that Natalie blamed him. She was grateful to him for taking the time to help her overcome her fears with Playboy, even after the terrible news. She just wished she could do something to help.

To her surprise Sam had called and asked if they could work together again. Maybe not so surprising, though. The woman still wanted to teach her horse, Roger, how to jump. Natalie didn't mind helping. It gave her something to do.

Three days after her breakthrough with Playboy she watched as Sam pulled up in a cherry-red pickup that reminded Natalie of her old truck, Lola. Sam was hauling a polished aluminum Platinum trailer that couldn't have been more than a year old.

Must be nice.

Now, now, Natalie counseled herself. She had learned early on that thoughts such as that seldom did any good. No need to get blue about the past. She preferred to focus on the future. On what might be down the road. Sure, she missed her old life, but she counted herself fortunate. With the sale of her truck, her good show horses and her fancy European car, she'd escaped the hospital without owing any medical bills.

Playboy was her future.

"Well, golly gee Moses and Mary, I haven't been out here in about a million years," Sam said as she unfolded her tall body from the confines of her truck. Natalie noticed then that the door said Galloping Girlz…as did the side of the trailer. "I didn't even know this place still existed."

Sam wasn't being snide, Natalie realized, once again admiring her beauty. Today she wore an emerald green shirt with rhinestones all over it and a matching headband. The day had dawned bright and sunny and that light caught the shirt and headband and set them aglow. Sam's hair flowed long and loose over her shoulders. It brought to mind Natalie's own long hair—back when she used to have it—and how much she missed being able to pull it back from her face instead of always having it brushing her cheek as it did now.

"I swear to God I rode my first pony at this place."

Natalie was glad to see her, if only to get an update on Colt and his nephew. She hadn't wanted to call. It seemed rude to poke her nose into something like that and so she hoped to find out more from Sam.

"Thanks so much for coming out." Natalie walked forward, wondering if she should offer her a hand or give the woman a hug. Sam seemed friendlier today, probably because Colt wasn't around. "I know you're busy."

"Oh, anything for Colt."

"Is this her?"

They both turned as Laney emerged from between one of the lean-to stalls and rushed forward. "Are you the Galloping Girl?"

Sam smiled, and her words were tinged with laughter when she spotted Laney's sparkling blue eyes. "We're called the Galloping Girlz, and I'm Sam, their leader."

"I know who you are. I saw your picture on your Facebook page."

"Oh, yeah? Did you Like us?"

"I did and I was hoping that maybe after you and Natalie are done you could show me some moves."

"I'll do better than that. Why don't you come out to our next practice at Reynolds's Ranch?"

If the woman had offered to buy Laney a new horse, the girl couldn't have seemed more thrilled. "Oh!" She turned to Natalie. "Can I go with you next time? Do you mind?"

"Not at all." Natalie glanced over at Sam, sharing a smile and thinking maybe the woman wasn't so bad after all. "You'll have to ask your parents first. I don't think they'd want you standing on your head on the back of a horse without knowing about it first."

"I'll ask, but they won't care."

Natalie's smile slipped a notch. She'd noticed Laney's parents weren't often around. Once, when she'd met Laney's mom, she'd spotted the glint of something silver in the woman's purse. A flask. She could smell the alcohol on her breath, too. Laney had seemed humiliated.

"You should still ask."

"I'll go text her right now." And she was off, heading back to the tiny wooden locker that served as a storage unit to hold all of Laney's secondhand tack—much of it having been Natalie's at one time.

"Nice kid." The smile lingered in Sam's eyes. "Reminds me of myself when I was younger."

"She's a heck of a rider, too." Natalie felt another twinge of melancholy. Jeez. What was with her today? "All the natural ability in the world. If I still had my lesson horses I'd be teaching her to jump."

"Speaking of jumping, I've been working on those exercises you gave me."

"And?"

They headed back toward Sam's trailer. "He's not looking at anything I put on the ground now."

"Good. That's the first step, teaching him that things in front of him aren't scary."

"What about you?" Sam asked. "Have you been doing the exercises I gave you?"

Sam was something of a fitness nut. She'd texted Natalie a long list of exercises to do every morning. "I have." And she'd started her hippotherapy lessons, too, and between it all, she actually felt she might be improving.

"Are they helping?"

"Actually, I think they are."

"Good." Sam swung open the back of the trailer. "My only concern is that Roger trips a lot over the poles."

"That's okay. Just as long as he's not spooking or refusing. We can help him learn to be less clumsy."

"Oh, good, because I really want to teach this guy a new trick." She went to Roger's head, patted his neck. The small bay gelding turned as far as the trailer tie would let him. He was in the first stall, and Sam expertly unclipped and then turned the animal around. "Jumping through a flaming hoop has always been a dream of mine."

"Isn't that everybody's dream?" Natalie teased.

Sam met her gaze and laughed, and Natalie realized she liked this version of Sam. She was friendly and clearly willing to help.

"Probably not everyone's, but it's been one of mine."

"And I can help with that. I have poles here. Even a few jump standards if we decide to take him over some fences."

Roger stepped out of the trailer like a perfect gentleman. "You think?"

"Sure, why not? It'll be easier to work with him here than at Colt's place."

She spotted the way Sam's smile slipped a notch. They'd talked briefly on the phone about Colt and his nephew.

"Have you talked to him since the doctor appointment?" Natalie asked.

The smile fell completely away from Sam's face. "Yeah. Not good. They're sending Adam down to the children's hospital to see some kind of specialist."

As someone who'd spent more time than she cared to admit with specialists, Natalie didn't envy Colt or his sister, but most of all she didn't envy poor little Adam. One test after another. Needles. Scans. Conferences with doctors. And at the end of it all, more often than not, uncertainty. Or worse.

You'll never ride a horse again.

The words still had the ability to suck the wind from her chest.

Sam paused with Roger standing patiently by her side. "That poor man has been through so much already. The whole family has, and now this." She shook her head. "It just doesn't seem fair."

It took a moment for Natalie to follow Sam's train of thought. "I heard Colt's dad was sick for a while."

Sam's eyes scanned her own and Natalie could tell that wasn't what she'd meant at all. She glanced toward the makeshift arena, the change in angle setting off the blue of her eyes, before clucking at Roger and heading toward the riding pen.

"I've known Colt my entire life," Sam said.

Had she? Colt hadn't mentioned it, not that he should have, but Natalie had just sort of figured they'd met through the rodeo circuit.

"Did you grow up in Via Del Caballo?"

"Yup." Sam pointed south. "Right down the road. My mom and dad breed cattle. Where'd you grow up?"

"Down south, in the desert, the product of middle class parents who could barely afford my horse habit."

"And yet you still found fame and glory. They must be proud."

Natalie hesitated. "They were always very supportive, despite not understanding my obsession."

Sharp-eared Sam didn't miss a thing. "Were?"

"My dad took up flying once I was out of the house." Natalie took a deep breath. "One day they decided to head toward Lake Tahoe." She shrugged because, really, what else was there to say?

They had come to a stop outside the gate, Sam's

gaze capturing her own, the depth of compassion in them as deep as the ocean. "I'm so sorry."

And with those three words Natalie decided she and Sam would be great friends. "It's okay. I'm mostly over it."

"No." Sam's dark hair fell over one shoulder when she gave a shake of her head. "You never get over something like that."

No, you didn't, and it almost sounded as though Sam knew from experience, although Natalie didn't want to pry.

"So, anyway, enough about me. You ready to work?"

"In a second." Sam's eyes grew, if possible, even more serious. "I wanted to talk to you about Colt."

Uh oh.

Sam fiddled with the end of the lead rope. "The next few months, hell, maybe even years won't be easy on him."

"No. I suspect not."

"And Colt's not the kind of guy that will reach out for help."

"No?"

Sam shook her head. "It's not in his programming. His childhood left some scars that run pretty deep, scars that keep him from asking for anything." Sam shot her a knowing look that made Natalie wonder just how bad it could be. "Suffice it to say I'm worried about him. With all his upcoming commitments, plus his sick nephew, he might just run himself into the ground like he did before."

Natalie realized then what Sam was getting at. "You want me to tell him I don't want his help anymore."

"Not right away." Sam reached out and rested a hand on her arm. "I know how important this is to you, but if you'll let me, I'll help you instead. I'm not as good at training horses as Colt is, but I'm not bad, either. We can help each other."

Was this some sort of competition thing? Natalie wondered. A way to keep her away from Colt? Was that what this was all about?

But as she studied Sam's eyes, she doubted it. What she saw in the woman's face was deep-rooted concern.

"What happened before?"

Clearly, Sam didn't feel comfortable sharing certain aspects of Colt's past. Just as clearly, she wanted Natalie to understand.

"Back when Colt's dad was sick, it got pretty bad."

Natalie waited for Sam to gather her thoughts, perhaps to decide how much to reveal and how much to keep to herself.

"You know Colt was in the military, right?"

Natalie nodded. She'd heard that, but little else about his background, other than the fact he'd grown up on Reynolds's Ranch and had taken over the rodeo business once he'd been discharged.

"But you probably don't know that everyone hated his father. My mom said Hank Reynolds could charm a snake from the ground, but he was as rotten as a rattler. She's convinced he killed Abigail, Colt's mom, and covered it up."

"That's horrible."

Once again Sam shot her an appraising look. "You don't know the half of it." The breath she took seemed to clear her mind. "One time when we were thirteen,

Colt refused to take his shirt off to go swimming. He told me he was afraid of getting sunburned, but I saw the bruises on his arms. I even asked him about it. He said he'd fallen off a horse, but we all knew better. My mom said Abigail used to come into town so bruised up it looked like she'd fallen out of the back of a truck."

The strange thing was, Natalie didn't feel the least bit surprised. Somehow she'd known there was something off with Colt. Not something wrong, just something that made him view the world differently than others did. She'd assumed it had to do with his time in the military, but now she knew better.

"The man's a saint, though. When his dad had his stroke, Colt came back home to nurse him—not that his dad appreciated it. Gosh, he was terrible. Made Colt's life hell. At the same time Colt's sister was nursing her husband so he was helping her out watching Adam and taking care of the dogs."

"The dogs?" Natalie hadn't seen a dog at the ranch.

"Yeah." Sam seemed surprised. "Colt's sister owns a kennel." Her nose twitched. "Not a kennel-kennel. She specializes in military dogs. Rehomes them and stuff."

"I had no idea."

"Yeah. She lives less than a mile from Colt and so he was always running between the two places, and, for the first few months, filling in for his dad on the rodeo circuit. It would have been hard on a normal person, but Colt's the type to keep going until he drops. He got sick. Wouldn't rest. We all told him to take a break, but he never listened. His sister found him passed out in the kitchen one day."

"Passed out? What happened?"

"Stupid man had pneumonia. For a while there it was pretty scary."

He'd worked until he dropped. Literally. Why wasn't she surprised?

"Anyway, my point is he's got a lot on his plate."

"And you don't want to see him dragged down again." When she looked into the woman's eyes she could see the relief that Natalie understood.

She thought back to when she'd been in the hospital, to how difficult it'd been on her friends. She didn't have any family, but thanks to Jillian and Mariah she'd made it through. They'd been a tag team, though, and neither of them had had a sick relative at the time.

"I'll talk to him tomorrow."

Sam's smile was so genuine it eliminated any thoughts of competition. "Thank you."

Before Natalie could say another word she was wrapped in a hug. She forced a smile because no matter what she might tell Sam, she was disappointed she wouldn't be working with Colt anymore, and oddly enough, not just because of his expert horsemanship. No. She liked Colt, liked him in a way that took her by surprise given how distant he'd been at first.

"You'll see." Sam drew back. "You've made the right choice."

Then why did it feel so wrong?

Chapter Eight

Some days you're the windshield, other days the bug.

Today Colt felt like a bug. His sister had left at the crack of dawn to take Adam to see a specialist. He'd offered to go along, but Claire had insisted he stay behind. Somebody had to take care of the ranch, she'd said: feed the livestock, check on the dogs, turn out the horses. He had to prepare for the rodeo coming up this weekend, too, and Natalie was coming over for another training session.

Natalie.

He couldn't seem to get the dang woman off his mind. He kept flashing back to the image of her sitting atop Playboy, laughing. Truth be told, it was the memory of that smile that had helped him get through the past few days. Right now the last thing he probably needed was another horse to ride, but helping Natalie didn't seem like work. It seemed like something he should do, though God knew why.

She pulled up right on schedule, although a quick glance at the sky told him they might have to cut their ride short. Looked like rain. She'd dressed for it in a burgundy jacket that matched the blush of her cheeks. He liked that she was always on time. Punctual to a T, but as she exited her old rattletrap of a truck, her serious expression took him by surprise. To his complete and utter shock he admitted to himself he'd been looking forward to her smile. What a crazy, ridiculous, stupid thing.

"What's wrong?" he called.

He saw her brow lift, her pretty blue eyes flash with surprise. "What do you mean?"

"You look like you're about to visit a sick relative in hospital."

"Well, in a way, I am." She walked up to him and Colt wouldn't have been a man if he didn't notice how good she looked. Those eyes of hers were the same color as a bluebird's wings—a bright, vivid hue that seemed to shimmer in the light.

"How's your nephew?" she asked.

Colt had been dealing with his sister all week, trying for Adam's sake to act as if nothing had changed. He shrugged as he turned and began walking with Natalie toward the barn. The wind kicked up again, catching the underside of his black cowboy hat and trying to blow it off his head.

"He's too young to understand what's going on, but I guess that's a blessing."

Her eyes lost some of their luster. "Poor thing. He'll understand soon enough."

Colt's stomach seemed to drop to his toes as he thought of the future. "Right now all he can talk about is *Hawkman*, his favorite movie of all time, but it's just a matter of days before he figures it out. They're starting chemo next week."

She tipped her head to the side, her short blond

bangs falling across her forehead. "And the thought kills you."

Was it that obvious? "I'm just hoping it won't be as bad as it sounds." He took a deep breath. "You ready to get to work?"

She paused just outside the barn. "Actually, I'd like to talk to you about that." She fiddled with the edge of the black shirt she wore beneath her open jacket, one with rhinestones in the shape of a cross. "Colt, you have a lot going on."

"Yeah."

"Sam and I were talking the other day and we both think maybe I should take Playboy home, you know, just until things settle down. I know you've been asked to watch your sister's place while they deal with hospital visits and that you have some rodeo obligations you can't get out of. The last thing you need is another commitment."

That sounded like Sam talking. His well-meaning neighbor could be a pain in the rear. He didn't mind her and the girls coming over and using his arena, especially since they were now a part of his act, but Sam had been after him for years to settle down, and she made no secret of the fact that she'd like to settle down with him. He'd always discouraged her because even if he were the type to dive into a relationship, which he wasn't, it wouldn't be with Sam. It would be with someone like…

Nope.

Wasn't going to go there. Not now. Yet even though he counseled himself to do otherwise, he couldn't take his eyes off Natalie. She was like a talisman for good, a comic-book hero who'd been through hell—

and had emerged with a smile. She was the epitome of brave, and damned if he didn't admire her.

"Admit it, Colt," she added. "You don't need to be dealing with me."

"What I *need* is to be allowed to make my own decisions."

Her eyes widened just the tiniest bit, enough for him to realize the words had come out harshly. He pushed his hat back a bit, trying to get his emotions under control. This was exactly why he avoided relationships. He was no good at them. No good at holding on to his temper.

Like father, like son.

"Look. Sorry. I know you're just trying to be nice, but what I need right now is to keep doing what I'm doing, and that means working with Playboy. Riding is my therapy and Playboy's such a responsive horse he's a joy to ride. You picked a good one."

Though the cloud cover afforded less light than usual, he could see the way her eyes lit up. "You think?"

"He learns really quickly. I'm riding him on a drape now."

"A drape?"

He smiled. "That's Western talk for riding with no contact. You drape the reins. Once I get him good and broke like that I'll try him without the reins."

"You still think I should do this then? You think I'm capable?"

It was funny. Three weeks ago the last thing he'd wanted was to help her. Now felt like grasping on to his little project with both hands, especially when she stared up at him so endearingly. He'd never met someone with such grit and drive. The other day she'd been terrified, but she'd done what he'd asked. She'd put herself completely in his hands and he couldn't deny he liked the feeling.

"I have no doubt in my mind."

He hadn't realized how tense she'd been until he saw her shoulders drop. "Okay then." She lifted her head, her sparkling eyes filled with determination. "But you have to let me help you, too."

"Excuse me?"

She nodded firmly. "I want to lend a hand around here. Whatever you need. Feeding the horses. Dogs. Cats. Doing your sister's laundry. Whatever."

The proposition took him by surprise. Sure, they'd had offers from others, but that was different. They were all good friends. He didn't know Natalie all that well.

"You don't have to do that."

"Yes, I do. In fact, I insist."

"We have plenty of help already."

She took a step toward him and it made Colt want to retreat. It wasn't that she stood too close, it was more that whenever she came near he had to fight the crazy urge to close the distance and…touch her.

Not good.

"I know what it's like not to have much family to count on." She looked away for a moment and in her expression he saw memories flicker. There for all the world to see, he caught glimpses of sadness, long-ing and pain. When she'd gotten herself together she lifted her chin. "Times like these, you need to lean on whoever you can." Her fingers captured his and for a moment Colt couldn't think. "I hope you count me as a friend."

It took every ounce of his intellect to muster the words, "I do."

She smiled. That beautiful, sparkling grin that could lift the spirits of a man on the verge of a lethal injection.

"Good. Then no arguing." She squeezed his hand. "I understand your sister runs a kennel, and I just happen to be really good with dogs. We'll go over there after we're done with Playboy."

She turned toward the barn as if the conversation was over, and he supposed in a way it was. He knew resolve when he saw it, and Natalie had it written all over her face. It was then, right then as she walked away, that he decided she was unlike any other woman he'd met. A woman who had her own burdens to bear, but who still wanted to help a near stranger. A woman of courage and kindness who made him, just for the tiniest moment, wonder what it would have been like if he hadn't been raised by a bastard with no heart. A man who'd destroyed his belief in love. A man who had taught him one golden truth: the fewer people you had in your life, the fewer people who could hurt you.

Chapter Nine

He'd made huge progress with Playboy. Natalie marveled as she watched Colt work with her gelding. The gathering clouds and cooler temperatures would make most horses fresh, and yet Playboy acted like a seasoned veteran. It was windy, too, sharp gusts threatening to remove Colt's Stetson from his head. That, too, made horses difficult to deal with. Usually. Playboy hardly seemed to notice the way his black mane tangled in the breeze or how his tail wrapped around his back legs every once in awhile.

"He looks good," she called.

Her words must have been snatched by the wind because Colt didn't appear to hear. He stopped in front of her a moment later and crooked his finger, urging her to ride. In the old days she would have avoided it on a day like today, but watching him work with Playboy gave her confidence. Still, when it came time to place her foot in the stirrup, she hesitated.

You'll never ride again.

Yes, but she wore a helmet, and she could just as easily take a spill off a bicycle or a ladder or even stepping off a curb. So what if reinjuring her brain might lead to permanent long-term complications such as paralysis…or *worse*. She refused to live life as if she were Humpty Dumpty afraid to take a tumble off a wall.

So she mounted.

"Okay, so don't collect your reins."

Natalie forced herself to concentrate, thinking maybe the wind might have taken part of his words away. "What do you mean don't collect them? Don't hold them at all?"

"No." He placed a hand on his head to keep his hat from blowing off. "Hold them like you normally would, just don't collect the slack."

She nodded. It seemed contrary to everything she'd ever been told and everything she taught her students, but she did it anyway.

"Okay, send him out to the rail."

A quick glance toward the mountains revealed a band of rain headed their way, although the clouds above seemed to be moving slower than the wind on the ground. They would have to hurry, but that was okay. Riding with no contact left her feeling as anxious as the first time she'd ridden with Colt. What if a plastic bag blew in from nowhere and spooked her horse? How would she stop him?

"Just relax."

Easy for him to say. Still, she closed her eyes, willing her body to do as it was told, the familiar swing of her horse's legs calming her nerves.

"Now try a circle, but instead of using the reins, I want you to put your weight on the inside stirrup of the direction you're turning."

His words prompted her to look at him. He was a dark figure standing in the middle of the arena in his black hat and black jacket. Once again she wondered if she'd misheard him. Leaning into a circle also went against her teaching. Sit up straight, her coaches had always told her. Don't tilt left or right. She closed her eyes. She trusted Colt and so she did as he asked, surprised and pleased when Playboy changed directions.

"If he starts to act up or move too fast, don't be afraid to go to the reins," Colt instructed. "But use your voice first. We want him to start responding to your words as well as your body language."

She found it hard to lean in without getting really, really dizzy. Something to do with her inner ear, no doubt. Yet lean in she did, fighting back nausea, and Playboy did exactly as Colt had trained him to do in a matter of days. Amazing. She could feel Playboy move beneath her, and it was a revelation to realize she could sense where they were going even with her eyes closed. A lean right and she would be headed back to the gate. She opened her eyes to see if she was right, pleased to note she was. She tested herself again, leaning left and moving toward the left corner, never looking, and when she gauged herself close enough, she checked her progress. Right where she thought she would be. It must have been a sixth sense. With her eyes closed she became hyperaware of everything. The sting of wind on her cheeks. The smell of rain in the distance. The sound of Playboy's hooves in the sand.

"I don't have to touch the reins at all."

Colt nodded, but said nothing. He liked to keep his emotions behind a mask of indifference, she realized. Pretend as if he didn't care one way or the other how things went. Yet when she studied him, took in the way his face softened when he was pleased, or the way his shoulders relaxed when Playboy behaved, she could tell what he was thinking. It was very much like reading horses. You had to look at everything as a whole in order to glean what they thought.

"Do you want to trot?" Colt asked.

Just the thought sent a shot of adrenaline straight to her heart. She wasn't certain she should do it, and perhaps she shouldn't, not yet. But sooner or later she'd have to do more than walk, because if she couldn't muster the courage for that, well, there was no sense in any of it.

"Do you think I'm ready?"

"I think you have to try." His gaze seemed affixed to hers.

"Okay."

Good Lord. Her hands began to shake and her heart beat so quickly it affected her breathing.

In for a penny, in for a pound.

She braced herself before saying the word, "Trot," in as stern a voice as she could muster.

Playboy set off instantly.

She wanted—oh, how she wanted—to clutch at the reins, to pull them toward her and jerk her horse to a stop. It took everything in her power simply to sit there, to do as Colt instructed and lean when she wanted to change direction. And then, when the dizziness struck with a force that made her breakfast somersault in her stomach, to close her eyes…

And focus.

The dizziness faded. Calm returned.

"Keep your center of gravity," Colt instructed.

It was like riding on a sled, a bouncy one. Trotting

meant she had to keep her eyes closed all the time with only occasional glances to ensure she wasn't about to mow down Colt. If she'd thought walking made her sick, it was nothing compared to trotting, but she managed it somehow.

"Okay, now try a lope."

"What?"

"Do it."

She couldn't. No way.

He must have sensed what she was thinking because he said, "Go on. Just a few strides. You can pull him up immediately if you want."

You used to jump fences five feet tall.

Yes, before. And Colt didn't know about what she'd been told. He had no idea that if she fell…

Don't think about it.

She gave the command to lope before she could talk herself out of it, her stomach lurching when Playboy immediately did as she asked.

Oh, dear heaven.

She clutched the reins. She didn't tighten them, just held them in a firm grip. She needed to trust that Playboy would keep her safe and that he would listen to her. She peeked to make sure she wasn't headed for the arena rail, surprised when her stomach didn't flip and the dizziness didn't return. In fact, Playboy moved so slowly, his lope so smooth and easy to sit that the opposite happened. She found she could keep her eyes open.

"I just need to keep my eye up."

"Your what?" Colt called.

"It's a jumping term. I can't look down."

"There you go."

Yes, there she went. She tried turning her head, but that made her woozy, so she focused on staring between Playboy's ears, a smile coming to her face as she sat in the saddle and guided him with nothing more than her weight.

"Whoa." She backed up the word by leaning back.

The gelding listened, his back end dipping down as he all but skidded to a stop. Natalie couldn't help but laugh.

"That was incredible," she marveled.

She glanced at Colt. As usual, his face seemed impossible to read. Seemed. But she caught glimpses of his thoughts below the surface. He'd rocked back on his heels, his eyes a lighter shade of copper. His hands were relaxed now and one side of his mouth tipped up. He looked at her with what might have been called bored indifference, but beneath it all she spotted deep-rooted pleasure.

"I said you could do it."

She nodded, stretching back so she could pat Playboy's rump, her horse's ears flicking in response. "You were right."

Colt walked up to her, rested a hand on her thigh, and Natalie grew dizzy for a whole other reason. She stared down at where that hand rested, her senses clearly hyperaware because she could feel the heat of his fingers and the weight of his palm and the gentle swipe of his thumb against the surface of her jeans.

"Good job."

Rare praise. She knew that. Colt didn't hand out compliments easily. And here she was lying to him.

It was as if one of the clouds overhead had darkened and taken all the joy out of the moment. She knew she had to tell him the one secret she'd never told anybody. She just dreaded doing it.

Dreaded disappointing him.

SHE'D GONE QUIET.

Colt couldn't figure out if she was just tired from her ride or if he'd been too hard on her.

"Look, if I'm pushing you too fast, just say the word and I'll back off."

"No, no." She shook her head as she led her horse to the barn. The wind had kicked up even more, blowing her cropped hair across her brow. "It's not that."

So it was something else then. "If you'd rather not help me out at my sister's, that's fine. With the rain coming I wouldn't blame you for bugging out."

"No, I want to help."

She said little else as they escaped the wind, Colt glad for the shelter of his barn. He got busy untacking her horse. The scent of sweaty animal filled the air. Some might dislike the smell, he thought as he pulled the saddle from Playboy's back, but it soothed his soul. No matter how bad things had gotten with his dad, there had always been this—horses and the comfort of them. So he took his time, touching Playboy here and there as he removed the bridle and slipped a halter on his head, talking to him, being gentle.

Like he wanted to be gentle with Natalie.

"Ready?" she asked.

Her question brought him back from the brink of his thoughts or, more specifically, the memory of how hard it had been to stop himself from pulling her down off her horse. He'd wanted to kiss her after she'd conquered her fear of riding Playboy. He still wanted to kiss her.

"Let's go," he replied.

Something was eating at her, too, although what it was he couldn't fathom. Was she mad at him for pushing her so hard? He wouldn't blame her if she was. He had a tendency to do that. Got it from his dad.

Thoughts of his father made his own mood sour. "We'll take my truck."

The curtain of rain had slid over the mountains and into the valley. They would have a half-hour, maybe less, before they would get a soaking. Fortunately, Claire's kennels were mostly covered, but the outside runs weren't.

"We'd better hurry," he said with a nod toward the hills. "Rain's coming."

His sister's place wasn't far from his own. No more than a five-minute drive. That would come in handy in the future, although he definitely didn't want to think about it.

"How many dogs does your sister have?"

He shrugged. "It varies."

"And she rehomes them?"

Sam must have filled her in. "Marcus was in the Army, too. Part of a canine combat unit. When he was forced to come back home because of his illness he had to leave his dog behind. It was something Claire never forgave the military for. That dog had saved his life more than once, but to the Army a dog is a commodity, and so Zero was given to a new handler. Claire worked hard to change all that after Marcus died. These days she takes the dogs that are no longer viable commodities and reunites them with their former handlers. Failing that, she rehomes them."

Natalie had turned to face him, and even though Colt wasn't big on conversation, he found himself thinking he didn't like it when she sat there all quiet. He liked her animated. Talking. Happy.

And that was a bizarre thought.

"What about when the dog's tour of duty ended? The military wouldn't give them back to their handlers even then?" She asked.

"Nope." His hand tightened on the steering wheel remembering how much his brother-in-law had loved his dog, and how hard it had been on him when he was forced to leave it behind. "Claire moved heaven and earth to get the military to work with her. Congressmen, senators, even writing to the president of the United States. I think they got tired of hearing from her and that's why they gave in."

"Did she ever get her husband's dog back?"

It was a question he dreaded. Even after all these years the memory of that reunion evoked a near physical pain near his heart. "Yes, she did."

For the first time since Natalie had gotten off Playboy, she smiled. "That's great. A happy ending."

No. Not really, but she didn't need to know that. He decided not to share the rest of the story with her even though she might ask about Zero when she met the dogs.

"Why are you looking at me like that? What happened?"

"Like what?"

"As if you've lost your best friend."

Because he *had* lost his best friend when Marcus

died, and it blew his mind that she could read that on his face. "Nothing." Just then a flat splotch of rain hit the windshield, the liquid dilating to a half-dollar size. "Looks like we're going to get wet."

As a change of subject, it didn't work. "I can tell by your face that whatever you're thinking about, it wasn't good."

They'd reached his sister's house and he used the excuse to evade the subject. "Better move quickly." He shut off the engine.

But she didn't move, didn't answer, just stared at him, her gaze as blue as the wings of a butterfly. Rain began to pound on the roof, the first drops like the taps of military drums.

"Tell me what happened."

He didn't want to, he really didn't. Even now, two years later, he could still taste bile in his mouth.

"The dog didn't make it, did it?"

He jerked his face toward her. How in the hell had she picked up on that? "What makes you say that?"

Her eyes flicked over his face. "You're like a book. I can read you."

He drew back, unsure what to say because he'd had the same thought about her earlier. Her admission disturbed him, and not because he didn't like her ability to read him. No. What disturbed him was the way her admission made him feel. Pleased. Relieved. Curious despite himself. They had a connection, and the more time he spent in her company, the harder it was to fight it.

She was still staring at him, still waiting. He swallowed and forced his gaze ahead, away from her. If he stared at her...

"It was near the end of Marcus's life." His hands tightened on the steering wheel. *Focus on your words.* "Claire swears the news did him in. She had Zero's body exhumed so he could be buried with her husband. Marcus loved that dog and Claire knew it. When it was all over and done with she vowed never to have the same thing happen twice. That's how Combat Pet Rescue came into existence."

He dared to glance at her, saw tears in her eyes, and had to look away.

"My sister's a pretty remarkable woman."

With all she had been through—the sadness of their childhood, the death of her husband—Claire could easily have become doubtful and disillusioned. But instead she was the eternal optimist. She believed Adam would be fine. They would all be fine. She believed one day Colt would find love. He'd never been able to convince her otherwise. She didn't deserve what she was going through now.

"I'm sorry," Claire said softly.

"Not your fault."

He turned to look her in the eye and when he did, the urge to touch her made his fingers twitch. What the hell was it with her?

"No, not just about your sister and her dog. That, too, but I'm sorry for something else."

He watched her lips move, wondered if they would be as soft and sweet as she was. He needed to get out of the truck. Away from her. Before...

"Can it wait?" His vocal cords didn't want to work. He had to cough to clear his throat. "Those kennels are going to be a mess in a matter of minutes."

She looked about ready to cry again. He saw her

turn away, look out the passenger-side window for a second before she took a deep breath and faced him again. "I shouldn't ride."

"Not in this kind of weather, no. Nobody should ride in this."

"No. That's not what I mean."

"You mean because it makes you sick? That's okay. We'll work on that."

He saw her rake her bottom lip with her teeth as she shook her head. She looked him square in the eye and he saw it then, or perhaps he just finally understood. There was guilt in her eyes and sorrow maybe even a hint of defiance.

"My doctor told me never to ride a horse again."

Chapter Ten

Natalie watched Colt's profile. If he were a horse, he'd be on the verge of kicking out. He clutched the steering wheel as if he needed to hold on to something to keep from flying off the handle.

And then one word emerged. "Why?"

He spoke in a tone that was calm, but his body language told her he was anything but. His shoulders kept flexing, as did his fingers on the wheel.

"I could reinjure myself or…"

"Or?" he asked, his fingers finally relaxing, but only so he could drum them along the steering wheel.

"Or worse."

"Worse how?"

She took a deep breath. "I could die."

He expelled something that was half curse, half huff of anger. "Maybe you should explain to me exactly what the doctor told you."

She hated talking about it, but she forced herself to say the words. "It's called second impact syndrome. It happens after a severe concussion. It may take months for my brain to thoroughly heal or even years, or it might never be completely the same. The thing is there's no way to know and so if I reinjure myself

I could be dealing with mild symptoms, or the very worst kind."

"You mean death."

She nodded. "Dilated pupils, loss of consciousness and, yes, a high probability of death."

He concentrated on breathing in and out. She watched him and tried not to feel miserable. There'd been something in his eyes before she'd broken the news, something that had made her breath catch and her heart beat faster. Something that had made her want to tell him the truth.

She looked away, shook her head. She should have told him sooner. She knew that. She should have told him that first day they'd met, but if she'd done that he wouldn't have agreed to train her. And who could blame him? What kind of person would agree to re-teach someone to ride, someone who might fall at their feet and die?

Colt moved suddenly, slipping out the door before she could say another word, his jacket instantly speckled by the rain. She followed suit, racing around the front of the truck to catch up to him.

"Colt. Wait."

He ignored her. The dogs had started to bark. Or perhaps they'd been barking since they'd first arrived, but she'd been too deep in her own troubles to notice.

"I want to help."

He didn't say the word, but his answer was no. She could tell by the way he kept on walking. The way he wouldn't even look at her. The disappointment and disillusionment in his eyes stung her like a slap.

She'd blown it. She knew that, but she was there to help and help she would. So she followed. The kennels consisted of a long row of sheds to the left of the house. They reminded her of horse stalls except they weren't as big and the front sides were made of chain link so she could peer at the dogs pacing back and forth inside.

"The thing is I may be okay," Natalie persisted. Colt turned and stared at her. She tried not to flinch when she spotted the anger in his eyes. "It's an inner ear thing, a symptom of my original brain injury and so the doctors are thinking I'm still not healed up. But I think maybe I am. That I might have damaged my inner ear permanently. It might not be connected to my brain injury at all." She felt as if someone had let the air out of her. "There's just no way of knowing for sure, not even with all the CT scanners in the world."

He'd stopped in front of a shed, a feed room of sorts. When she said nothing further, he turned away again, heading inside the room. He went to the wall and pulled down a shovel. She did the same even though he didn't ask, didn't even notice, just opened the first kennel and went inside. The name Samson was written on a miniature whiteboard along the front. At least he hadn't told her to leave. Natalie went in after him. Samson looked to be a German shepherd, and he walked up to Natalie, tail wagging. She gave him a pat on the head before getting to work. Whatever Colt did, she did, too, all the while wondering if she should have kept her troubles to herself.

They moved to the next kennel. The next dog looked a lot like the first, but didn't seem as friendly. It hung back near the far end of the pen. "Will he bite?" she asked.

"No."

Well, he'd answered her. That was a good thing, but he was still angry. No, furious. And so she cautiously set to work. The dog—Juno, according to the name board—sat in the corner watching her as she scraped the concrete floor, filled the water bowl and then, per Colt's instructions, fed the gorgeous animal.

"Why do his ears look funny?"

She didn't expect him to answer. She could tell the fire of his anger still burned bright, but he did. "He's a Belgian Malinois."

She'd never heard of the breed. "He's so quiet."

"They're all like that." He turned and went back to work on the next kennel. She did the same without being told. There were six dogs in all, two Goldens and four Malinois.

"Is your sister trying to find them homes?"

They were putting away the tools, Colt's body language still radiating displeasure, but he didn't seem as angry as before. She realized then that she'd picked the perfect time to tell him. He'd been able to work his anger off. At least to the point that he didn't want to kill her anymore.

"She doesn't need to try. People come to her."

"You mean their former handlers?"

He snapped closed the lid of the dog-food container. "Sometimes, if they've been discharged. If not, civilians are allowed to adopt them, sometimes even local law enforcement agencies. It just depends."

She stared down the row of kennels. Even over the sound of the rain on the metal roof she could hear a few of them crunching their dog food, although more than one stared at them intently. The Malinois looked almost exactly like German Shepherds, right down to the brown-and-black coats and piercing, golden eyes.

Eyes like Colt's.

"I'm so sorry."

She hadn't meant to blurt the words, but as she'd watched him standing there, darkness in his eyes, she'd known she couldn't just pretend as if nothing had happened. The undercurrent of tension was the elephant in the room. They couldn't avoid the subject—not if they wanted to remain friends. Correction. Not if she wanted *him* to remain a friend. She was afraid he was counting the minutes until he would never have to see her again.

"Colt?"

"I don't want to talk about it."

She *had* to make him understand. "It was wrong of me, I know that." She went into the feed room. "But honestly I didn't think it would matter."

"Didn't think it would matter?"

The furious tone of his words couldn't be mistaken.

"You didn't think I would care if you came off a horse and died?"

"But I didn't. And I won't."

"You're damn right, you won't. I'm through helping you."

She'd known he might say that. yet the words still hurt. "Please tell me you don't mean that."

"What else haven't you told me?"

Beneath his cowboy hat his eyes had gone nearly as dark as his pupils. She took another step toward him. "I've told you everything."

He didn't look as though he believed her. He just stood there, as immovable as a stone, eyes just as cold.

"Would you like to talk to my neurosurgeon?"

His mouth tightened before he said, "Why? So he can tell me not to let you ride? Because you know that's what he'd say."

Her gaze dropped because she knew he was right. She should have been honest with him. Should have told him the situation right from the beginning.

"I had nothing left."

Only as she said the words did she finally comprehend her actions. How messed up was that? She took in a deep breath for courage and looked him in the eyes.

"I was in the hospital for months. When I got out I was up to my eyeballs in debt and barely able to walk. All my clients had jumped ship, and I had no place to stay and nothing ahead of me but a long recovery." Just talking about it brought it all back. The fear. The sorrow. The hopelessness. "And then I went out to the barn to see my horses. I knew I was going to have to sell them all, and so I went out to take pictures of them, but when I entered Playboy's stall..." She took another step closer to Colt, so close now she could feel the heat radiating off his body. "He turned and looked at me, and then he nickered and I just couldn't do it. I wrapped my arms around him and buried my head in his mane and I knew that somehow, some way, I'd keep him. That I'd ride him again. That'd I compete on him again one day."

She felt the familiar burn of tears on her lashes. There had been a time when all she seemed to do was cry. A time when she'd wondered if it might not have been better if she'd died. Then she'd realized she did have something to live for, and it'd brought her back from the brink of depression.

"My little horse is the reason I forced myself to get better. The reason I walk as well as I do now. He got me through one of the worst times of my life and, to be honest, it's not just that I want to ride him. I *need* to ride him."

She wasn't certain her words had gotten through to Colt, but she'd said her piece. Natalie was angry with herself when she felt a tear drop to her cheek. She brushed it away, calling herself a fool as she stared down at her toes. She couldn't fault him for being angry. She would be, too, if she learned one of her riding students had deceived her in such a way.

He started to move past her again and Natalie was unable to contain her disappointment, which was why she snatched at his hand. Why she tugged him toward her, silently asking him not to leave, begging him with her eyes to understand.

"It was wrong of me," she admitted, holding his gaze. "But I needed to ride. I needed to be with my horse. I needed him to help me get through some of the worst times of my life. I couldn't sell him and I couldn't let him sit in a stall and rot, and so I did something about it. Good or bad. Right or wrong. That was my decision."

She glanced down at their hands. His fingers were so big and rough compared to her own. His nails were short but well kept and she wondered, just for a moment, what they would feel like against her skin…

That thought came out of nowhere, so startling that her gaze shot to his as if he might somehow have gleaned what she'd been thinking. He didn't blink and his eyes had gone dark. His hand tightened around hers.

"I'm sorry," she heard herself say. She squeezed his hand back and then before she could talk herself out of it, leaned toward him. He didn't move away, didn't lean into her. He didn't move at all. A million thoughts floated through her mind. How broad his shoulders were. How, despite his brusque demeanor, his eyes always had a hint of kindness in them. Her free hand lifted to his cheek. "Do you understand?"

What are you doing? She asked herself.

Asking him to kiss me, she admitted. She wanted to touch him and hold him and tell him without words how sorry she was for keeping her health problems from him and how badly she felt about his own terrible past. She could see in his eyes that he'd been thinking about it. That he knew how important horses were to her. She'd found a kindred spirit.

He didn't resist as she moved toward him, but neither did he make it easy on her. She had to stand on the very tips of her toes in order to press her lips against his. One second, two. She tipped her head the other way, her tongue slipping out to swipe his lower lip.

And it changed.

One moment he was immovable. The next he'd jerked her up against him.

"I do understand," he muttered against her lips.

His hands splayed wide as he pressed them against the small of her back, and his head lowered. She came down on her heels. His mouth opened and then they were touching in the most intimate of ways, a hot caress that allowed her to taste him. Honey, chocolate and just a hint of coffee.

Perfect.

His lips fit her mouth seamlessly. He angled his head just right. His mouth was sweet and warm and she had a distant thought that she'd been waiting for his kiss her entire life.

His hands began to shift, moving down her back and then slipping beneath her jacket. The warmth of his fingers made her tremble, or maybe it was something more, something that warmed her middle and sent shivers down her legs and then back up her thighs.

He pulled back. They stared down at each other for a moment. Natalie felt his fingers slip away and she knew from the look in his eyes that he'd come to his senses.

"That was a mistake." His voice was a near growl, making him sound as if he'd gone from beguiled to betrayed. "I should get you back to my ranch."

Never had she been so confused. She wanted to capture his hand again, to tell him to not leave, but she was afraid she'd already pushed him too far.

"Colt, please."

He left the feed room as if the place were on fire. She stayed behind, wishing for just a moment that she wouldn't have to ride in the truck with him.

The rain began to pour even harder. The noise on the tin roof nearly drowned out the sound of his truck when it started up.

I won't ever see him again.

The thought nearly brought her to tears once more. She liked him. A lot. Too bad he no longer liked her.

Chapter Eleven

The drive back to Colt's place was one of the most uncomfortable journeys of Natalie's life, despite being so short. He didn't say a word. Didn't look at her. Didn't acknowledge her existence. When she stepped out of his vehicle and into the rain, he sped off— heading goodness knows where—without so much as a goodbye.

She sat there, her short hair capturing the downpour, strands acting as miniature drain spouts, and watched as his taillights faded behind a mist of rain.

"Damn, damn, damn."

She thought about following him. Thought about texting and asking if she should make arrangements for Playboy. Wondered if she should just wait for him to come back.

She didn't. She'd already made him mad. She didn't think hanging around would endear her to him any further.

HE DIDN'T CALL. Didn't text. Natalie debated about what to do up until the moment her friend Jillian knocked on her door.

"You going to let me in?" Jillian asked when she spotted Natalie peering through the curtain.

In a flash Natalie knew Colt had told her friend what had happened.

"Well?" Jillian asked.

Too late to dodge the bullet now. Reluctantly, Natalie opened the door. Jillian peered at her through green eyes that blasted anger. "You were told never to ride again?"

Just as she expected. *That* cat was out of that bag.

"Good to see you, too," she said, opening the door wide so all her neighboring tenants wouldn't get an earful. She'd been looking for cheap when she'd first gotten out of the hospital. She'd found it in a not-so-nice part of town, the upside being that she wasn't far from Via Del Caballo Stables. The downside was that she shared a parking lot with low-lifes, druggies and newly minted college graduates. She considered it a temporary stop in her life, but that didn't mean she had to like the single-story complex with the thin walls and the drive-up-to-your-front-door parking.

"I mean, come on, Natalie," Jillian said, moving past her, the rhinestones on the pockets of her jeans catching the light. "You never thought to mention that to me or Wes or Colt? No wonder he's so livid."

Livid? He hadn't seemed livid when she'd kissed him.

She'd kissed him.

She still couldn't believe she'd done that. But he'd liked it. She'd reviewed what had happened at least fifty times through an entire sleepless night, and she knew she wasn't mistaken. He'd felt something. She'd felt it, too.

"I was going to tell you."

She saw Jillian glance around her apartment. It'd been nearly a year since her wreck and Natalie wondered if Jillian did the same thing she did, comparing the place to the cottage Natalie used to live in at Uptown Farms. Cottage. She huffed inwardly. More like a house. Compared to the seven hundred square feet she had now, Uptown Farms had been a palace.

"Were you?" Jillian asked.

She flicked her angular bob, the black strands coming to rest across her cheeks. Natalie wished she could appear as stylish as her friend with her short hair.

"For goodness sake," Jillian added. "I was there that day Playboy took off on you. What if you'd fallen off then? What if you'd died on the ground in front of me? What then?"

Natalie splayed her hands in mute apology. "I heard it all from Colt. Please. I don't need to hear it again. I know what I did was wrong."

Jillian's black brows rose nearly all the way to her hairline. "Wrong and selfish and foolish to boot."

Natalie didn't argue. While her health was a personal issue, what she'd done was like going to a doctor and neglecting to mention a heart condition when she knew she might get surgery. Ethically, she should have told the professional she was working with. The question was, how to make it up to her friend…and to Colt.

"I can't stop riding, you know." The words came out of her mouth unbidden. "I told Colt I needed to ride my horse, and I meant it."

Jillian took a seat at the pitifully small kitchen table.

The chairs were plastic with aluminum legs that had long since lost the caps on the feet. They made a scraping noise on the floor as Natalie settled into a rickety chair opposite her friend.

"Goodness, what a mess." Jillian shook her head and leaned back. "Colt wants you to take Playboy back. He says he won't be party to you killing yourself. He said to do it this weekend while he's at the Golden State Rodeo."

"He wants me to take him back?" She'd known it was coming, but it still didn't make it any easier to bear.

"Sooner rather than later."

She nodded, wracking her brain for how she could fix things. "Is Sam performing with him?"

Her friend cocked a head at her curiously. "Not this weekend. Not until they get the new act sorted out. Why?"

"Maybe Sam will help with Playboy."

"Sam will take Colt's side."

Yeah, she probably would—the other reason Natalie had lain awake and tossed and turned. She might be foolish for wanting to ride again, but she wasn't so foolish as to ride without someone's help. Not anymore. Just the few short weeks she'd spent with Colt had been immeasurably helpful. Proof that she should keep going with someone on the ground. Chances were she could find someone through word of mouth, but that would take time.

"I guess I'll have to go it alone for a little bit."

"No."

Jillian sounded so adamant and so horrified Natalie knew she'd break her friend's heart if she went behind her back. Could she bear to lose another person she cared about?

No.

"Any word on Colt's nephew?" Natalie asked. Maybe a change of subject would help clear her mind.

"They've started aggressive chemo, to be followed by some kind of immune suppression therapy. They have to kill all the blood cells." Jillian's green eyes turned sad. "Good ones with the bad. Poor little kid won't know what hit him."

And Natalie worried about never riding a horse again. Suddenly, her problems seemed so small.

"Maybe I should send him a present or something."

Jillian nodded. "Adam and his mom will be down south for a few weeks. He'll be allowed to come home once his first round of chemo is finished, but I imagine he'll be feeling pretty poorly by then."

She couldn't even imagine. "Sometimes life doesn't seem fair."

"No." Jillian leaned forward again. "It doesn't."

Colt must be beside himself. Watching Adam go through that... Well, that was something she wouldn't wish on her worst enemy.

"What hospital is he at?"

"Children's Hospital Los Angeles."

She'd heard of the place. She'd ridden in a Grand Prix that benefited their oncology department back when she'd been Natalie Goodman, international equestrian superstar. They'd brought a few of their kids out to the competitions. Sickly, wheelchair-bound adolescents who had broken her heart.

Colt's nephew would be one of them. It made her feel ill.

"I just wish there was something I could do."

Jillian clearly wished the same thing. "We're working out a schedule to help take care of Claire's animals."

"Can you put me down for a rotation? Colt might be mad at me, but he can't stop me from helping his sister. Besides, he showed me how to care for the dogs so I know what to do."

Natalie went back to staring at her again. "I don't know. I'd have to ask Colt."

Of course she would. And Colt would say no. And of course she'd be banned from helping him in any way.

"There has to be something I can do."

"If I was you I would just work on getting Playboy out of there. And for everyone's sake, promising not to ride."

The sick feeling flipped her stomach again. "I need to ride."

"Natalie, you could die."

"So could you." She glanced out the window of her apartment, at the cars lined up like cows at a feeder along the front of the complex. At the rooftops of downtown Via Del Caballo. At the mountains beyond. The rain had subsided, leaving behind a sky so crystalline it was like the bottom of a glass. She turned back to her friend. "You could die crossing the street."

Jillian's green eyes flared. "The difference being the street won't rear up and fall over on me."

"Playboy won't do that to me, either."

Jillian's petite hands reached out to her friend's. "Natalie, please. I'm not asking you to give up horses. You're a dynamite trainer. That's what you should be doing." She gave Natalie's hands a squeeze. "I've heard of trainers that never ride. They hire assistants."

Natalie couldn't contain her huff of laughter. "Assistants. As if I could afford that."

"Not now." Jillian's eyes conveyed how much it meant to her that she heed her advice. "Once word gets out that you're back on your feet, people will want you for a trainer again." But then Jillian's expression grew curious. "And that brings me to my next question. Why haven't you told people you're training again?"

"I have told people."

"Not everyone." Jillian's eyes narrowed. "You've taken on locals and that's it. You haven't done anything to advertise your services. It's almost like you're in hiding."

Frankly, she hadn't given it much thought. "People know I'm back. The people I care about."

"You used to be one of the best hunter/jumper trainers in the United States. Your talent is wasted on locals."

"Not on Laney."

Jillian's face softened. "Laney being the exception. She could really be something if you'd only put a little effort into getting back in the game."

Back in the game. She hadn't believed she was out of it.

"Promise me you'll think about it." Jillian stood. "That you'll stay off Playboy for a while. Just until you've had time to think things through."

She didn't want to promise her friend anything, but she did anyway. "I promise."

She didn't know if she would keep that promise,

but their conversation had given her an idea. A really great idea. One that might earn her forgiveness. Maybe. Even if it didn't, it would lift little Adam's spirits—and that meant she had to try.

IT TOOK COLT a week to calm down. It wasn't that he was mad at Natalie. It was more that he was angry with himself for getting sucked into helping her.

And kissing her.

That was the hardest thing of all to forget. Sure, he didn't live like a saint. There'd been the occasional fling out on the road. But that was just it. They'd been quick and easy to forget. He hadn't been able to forget Natalie.

She didn't make it easy for him, either. Sam revealed that she'd been coming around on weekends and helping out. She'd taken Playboy home, so she had no reason to drop by, but both Sam and Jillian sang her praises. He'd be a jerk not to acknowledge that he appreciated her help.

So as he arrived at Children's Hospital Los Angeles two weeks later, he was still thinking about her and wondering if she'd ridden at all. He refused to ask. It'd probably get back to her somehow, and he didn't want Natalie to know that he cared. He didn't care.

"How's my big guy?" he asked as he entered Adam's room.

"Uncle Colt!"

He went to his nephew's bed, trying not to blanch at the sight of his pale skin, grabbing his foot beneath a light blue hospital blanket and giving it a tug. He had to force himself to smile as he turned toward his sister who sat by Adam's bed.

"Here," he said, thrusting flowers at her. "Happy Mother's Day."

Claire stared at the flowers in surprise, her eyes filling with tears before she took them from him with a nearly inaudible, "Thanks."

Hell of a way to spend her Mother's Day, he thought. Damn it. His sister had spent far too many days next to the sickbed of a loved one. He'd always believed in God, but it was hard to keep the faith when he had to watch people suffer over and over again.

"How was your drive?" she asked as she set the flowers down on the brown Formica table by Adam's bed.

"Fine," he said, moving around to the bed's other side. He'd been cleared for admittance by the nurse who ran the floor. His nephew's white blood cell count was still high enough that his immune system could resist any bugs Colt might inadvertently bring into the room, although he'd been strictly forbidden to touch or kiss the boy, and he'd had to scrub himself down with antibacterial gel.

"Long," he added. "I'll be glad when rodeo season ends."

He felt as though he'd been on the road nonstop for days. His rodeo commitments were impossible to get out of. The dates had been booked years in advance and finding a replacement was nearly impossible. Not that he hadn't tried. He'd rather spend every moment by his nephew's side, but it just wasn't possible.

"How are you, bud?" he asked his nephew, taking

a seat in a chair with bright blue cushions and the permanent indent where hundreds of rear ends had sat.

Adam's shoulders beneath the pastel yellow hospital gown lifted up and down. He'd had a tough time of it. It killed Colt every time he heard the stories of how Adam cried when they injected the chemo into his veins. He'd gone from a naive kid who equated his sickness to a bad cold, to a little boy who sensed something serious had happened. It scared the you-know-what out of his nephew. Colt could see the fear in his eyes. Tore him up every time.

"Thanks for coming by," his nephew said softly.

"Are you kidding? I'd be here more often if I could."

He caught his sister's eyes. The sadness in them couldn't be mistaken, nor could the worry. She looked especially pale before a backdrop of gray walls and gray décor. Not even the sunshine beaming in from the window behind her could add color to her cheeks.

"I appreciate all you've been doing, Colt. I know the dogs can be a real pain."

He hoped his smile eased her worry. "Actually, I've had lots of help. Sam won't be joining my act until the Fourth of July shows, so she's been at the ranch. So has Jillian and a few other people."

"Like Natalie?"

The worry had faded into a teasing glint. Colt hated to burst her bubble so he kept quiet about recent developments. "Yes, like Natalie."

He had no idea why his sister seemed convinced he should be interested in the woman, but if thinking about him getting involved in a romantic relationship helped take her mind off other things, so be it.

"I was surprised when she called today and asked if she could come by."

He would have fallen out of his chair if he hadn't been in one of those thickly padded wooden monstrosities common to hospital rooms. He couldn't keep his boots from slamming down on the floor, though.

"Coming by?"

Claire had straightened, too, green eyes wide. "Yeah. I thought you knew."

And there it was. The reason why he should have told her about Natalie, although who would ever have thought she'd overstep the bounds by driving down and visiting his nephew.

"What time is she supposed to be here?" Maybe he could leave beforehand.

"Any minute now. She wanted to make sure you were here, too." Claire shoved her long hair over one shoulder. "I'll be honest though, it never occurred to me—"

His sister's startled gaze caused him to turn toward the door. He had to blink to make sure his eyes weren't deceiving him. Hawkman, hero of the DC Comics world, stood in the entryway. Or the actor who played him, anyway. Rand Jefferson, household name, recreating his big-screen persona. Colt wasn't prone to gawking, but he felt his jaw drop. Behind him Adam gasped, and Colt knew his nephew had seen him, too, especially when he heard Adam say in a reverent tone, "Hawkman."

Someone appeared from behind the actor. Natalie. She gave Colt a smile, one full of pride, smugness and something else, something like a plea for forgiveness.

"Hello, young knight," Hawkman said, coming into the room in full comic book regalia, which meant the most ludicrous set of wings Colt had ever seen. They were huge. And…feathery…and barely fit through the door. But that wasn't all. He was shirtless but for crisscrossed straps that did nothing to conceal his six-pack abs. He wore green tights that should have looked ridiculous on a man, but didn't, and he carried some kind of hammer-like mace thing, but for some strange reason it all worked. "I am told you are ill."

When Colt looked back at his sister, he could see that her eyes had filled with amusement. His nephew's eyes had gone wide, too, but that wasn't what held Colt's gaze. What kept him riveted was the transformation Adam had undergone. The sadness had fled, and the fear, too. His shoulders, once bent by exhaustion, were straight.

Colt saw the boy mouth a single word. "Cool."

It was. Colt glanced at Natalie and he knew that somehow she'd orchestrated the whole thing. In that moment he could have kissed her, although to be honest, he'd been wanting to kiss her for days.

Chapter Twelve

As ideas went, it had been one of her better ones, Natalie thought. Adam had positively lit up when Rand, aka Randy, had walked into the room.

"How in the heck did you arrange this?" Claire asked. They'd been nudged into the corner of Adam's room to make way for hospital staff, doctors and, even more important, other young patients who wanted to meet one of the world's best-known superheroes, Hawkman.

"With the help of the hospital, of course." Natalie smiled at one of the nurses. The woman in the brightly colored smock seemed about ready to swoon when she caught sight of Rand Jefferson's face. "Happy Mother's Day, by the way."

Claire's expression softened. "Thanks."

"Sorry you have to spend it here."

Claire nodded, eyes catching on Randy. "At least the view's improved."

Yes, it was a good view, Natalie thought, watching Colt. He wore no hat today, but he still managed to appear as if he'd ridden in from the range in his tan button-down, jeans and cowboy boots.

"Did the hospital arrange for Rand?"

"No, actually." Natalie smiled, liking the way Colt looked without his hat. He had the makings of sideburns, she realized, wondering how she'd missed that before. "That was me."

"You?"

"I've known Randy for a long, long time."

"You're kidding!"

Natalie nodded. "We went to high school together." She glanced at her old friend with his thick head of blond hair and buff body. "The product of a Southern California public school education."

The two women went back to staring at the scene by Adam's bed. Randy had always been good-looking, but his big break playing a peacekeeper from another planet had forced him to bulk up…*a lot.* The result was a godlike creature that Natalie barely recognized and that made most women swoon…such as that nurse. Not Natalie, though. She'd known Randy too long. It was hard to think romantically about a man you'd seen cry like a baby when he'd had his tonsils removed.

Colt seemed impressed by her friend, too, and at least he was smiling now. That was better than before. He was surrounded by hospital staff, each of whom gawked at Randy, and each of whom had their picture taken. They were wheeling their patients in and out. Adam held court from his position in bed, and Natalie couldn't help but smile when she spotted the look of pride on his face as yet another sick child was introduced to his new friend.

"I can't believe you know him," she heard Claire murmur.

"Actually, I helped him get his big break."

Claire's brows lifted as she waited for an explanation.

"Couple of years ago Randy was still waiting for his acting career to click. We'd kept in touch, especially since we both ended up moving north. He'd had a few bit parts on sitcoms and commercials and whatnot, but nothing substantial. One of my clients at Uptown Farms was a talent scout. She happened to mention they were looking for a Nordic-type actor to play in a big-budget film, and I thought of Randy. Now he's—" she made air quotes with her fingers "—Hawkman." She tried not to smirk because it just seemed insane. While she'd been out flat dealing with her head injury her friend had suddenly turned into a movie star. "He's promised to name his first-born after me."

"No!"

"Not really, but he tells me all the time that he owes me big, so this is payback. Well, a little bit of payback, he says. I'm supposed to go to his next *Hawkman* movie premiere, and to be honest, I'm really looking forward to that."

Claire's eyes studied her friend. "Well, I'm surprised you didn't volunteer for the job of surrogate mother." A smile tilted her lips. "I think a lot of women would have."

Natalie laughed. "No. There was never anything like that between us. He was always just my friend, the actor. To tell you the truth, my friend Jillian dated a bigger star. Well, maybe not so big now that Hawkman's such a huge success."

"Jillian, yeah. She dated Jason Brown."

She'd forgotten for a moment that Claire knew Jillian, too.

"Yeah. And we all know how that turned out." Natalie made a moue of distaste. "I told Randy if he ever treated a woman the way Jason Brown treated Jillian, I would kill him. Anyway, when I called him and told him about Adam he was only too happy to swing by."

"Well, it made Adam's day." Claire's words were a near sigh. Clearly she'd fallen under Randy's spell, too, and that prompted Natalie to study her for a moment. Colt's sister was gorgeous with her long black hair and green eyes and Natalie wondered if she and Randy might make a couple, but then she quashed the idea. She doubted Claire had time for romance. Her gaze shifted to Adam, barely visible between all the people that crowded his room. Not for a long time.

They'd been forgotten in their corner. "He's a really nice guy. He'd had no idea about my wreck, what with all this." She waved her hand around at the crowd of people. "I guess he's got his choice of new projects, but he's signed on to do two more *Hawkman* movies. Even with all that, his first question to me was how he could help." She smiled at the memory. "He's just always been great. The same old Rand I remember from high school, except he went by his real name back then, Randy Jones. I don't think I'll ever be able to call him Rand."

She and Claire shared a smile, but as Natalie went back to watching the scene in front of them, her smile faded. Jillian had been right. She'd been avoiding her old friends. Randy had made that clear. He'd asked her why she hadn't called and told him about her accident, and then made her feel guilty about missing the premiere of his movie. It'd reminded her that she'd had a life before the wreck and that Randy was a part of it. She was one of his oldest friends. It had brought her to tears and it'd made her wonder—why *hadn't* she called?

Because she'd been hiding.

The realization that Jillian had been right prompted her to make other calls, too. She'd been admonished by a few, not in a bad way, just gently chided. They'd missed her. One—a former client—flat out admitted she'd felt pushed away and so had given up trying to help. Mostly, though, she'd been made to feel loved and missed by friends and other professionals in the hunter/jumper world. She'd been humbled by the realization that she hadn't been forgotten. Humbled and rejuvenated. Time to quit pouting. Time to start rebuilding her business. Time to get back in the game. She didn't need to ride for that.

But she wanted to. Oh, how she wanted to.

She'd done some serious soul searching during the past two weeks. Colt and Jillian had forced her to take a good, hard look at her life choices. Was riding that important to her? Or was she being ridiculous? In the end it'd come down to one thing: passion. Horses were her life. If she couldn't ride it would be like tearing out a piece of her heart. She had no family to worry about. No kids to try and support. Nobody but her friends would mourn her passing, and while she would hate to put them through that, it was no reason not to at least try.

A camera flashed. It brought Natalie back to the present. One of the nurses faked a swooning heroine pose in Randy's arms, and the whole room erupted into laughter as yet another fan was born.

"That's going on Facebook," Claire said.

"Not just Facebook, the Twitterverse, too, I bet." She nodded with her chin toward the scene in front of them. "So far, so good. At least your brother no longer looks like he wants to kill me, unlike the last time we were together."

She felt rather than saw Claire's puzzled stare. "What do you mean?"

A glance at Colt's sister's face revealed what Natalie had suspected. She didn't know about their argument. "Colt and I sort of had a disagreement."

"I knew it! I could tell something was going on. What about?"

She wondered for a second how much to tell her, but then decided to hell with it. She needed an ally and Claire just might be it. Goodness knew Jillian and Wes had taken Colt's side. If it were up to them they'd cover Natalie with Bubble Wrap for the rest of her life.

"I neglected to tell him something and he got a little angry about it." Colt's sister tipped her head as she waited for an explanation. "Something kind of important."

"Such as?"

Natalie liked Claire, and it brought home just how much when she felt a rush of guilt at the thought of confessing her sins. Oh, well.

"I was told never to ride again." She said the words in a rush, as if getting them out quickly might help. "As in to never, ever climb on a horse again."

"Why not?"

Okay, big breath. She still hated to say the words. "If I fall off, odds are, I might die."

No response. Natalie watched as Claire's eyes went wide. "Why?"

"There's no way to know if my brain is completely healed. They can't just open me up and look, and scans can only tell them so much. The fact that I still have equilibrium problems is a big red flag. I could wait for my ear problems to go away, or I could just take the plunge. Since I don't want to stay off horses for what could be years, I decided to take my chances."

"Oh my goodness."

That pretty much summed it up. "Colt didn't take the news well."

"No. I imagine he wouldn't." Claire tipped her head toward her brother. "He's kind of a stickler about safety. Stems from our childhood when my dad would beat the you-know-what out of him for failing to check a girth or buckle a chin strap."

That took her by surprise. "You mean the same man that put Colt up on a runaway horse was a zealot for safety?"

Claire's gaze shot to her own. "Colt told you about that, did he?"

Natalie nodded, but she wasn't certain Colt's sister saw it. Her gaze had fixed once again on her son, and Natalie could see emotions gallop across her face as she watched the scene in front of her. "That was the least of our father's sins."

Should she push her? "I heard he was a bit of a drinker."

Claire's gaze hooked her own again. "A bit?" She huffed. "He was drunk more than he was sober."

That made Natalie draw back in surprise. "Really?"

Claire's expression changed in a way that Natalie didn't understand, not at first anyway. The woman slipped in front of her again, blocking her view. "If I tell you something, you've got to promise me you won't tell Colt that I told you."

That sounded ominous. "Sure."

Claire glanced over her shoulder at her brother. The sadness draped over her face again, her green eyes turning as sad as sparrows.

"My dad was more than a bad drunk." She took a deep breath and paused a moment before saying, "He was a piece of work that would beat Colt within an inch of his life for the slightest infraction."

Natalie wasn't surprised. "I'd heard he could be rough."

"He was way more than rough. He'd do…other things. Like that deal with the runaway horse. He didn't do it because he was drunk. He did it because he was mean. Evil. Some days I swore that man was possessed by the devil. He'd turn that temper on me sometimes, but Colt was always there to run interference for me, and for Chance, at least until he left for the Army."

Why had Colt gone back home to nurse him then? Why had he taken over his business? Sure, she'd known there was some tension between them. She'd sensed that. But this? This she would never have figured.

"Once, my dad got so angry at Colt he picked up a bridle and whipped Colt with it. The reins tore through Colt's denim shirt. It left scars. Physical ones and emotional ones. He still has them."

Natalie asked the question burning on her mind. "Why did he come back?"

"You mean to nurse our dad when he was sick?" Claire swiped her hair out of her face again. "I was dealing with my own problems. My husband was sick. He died when Adam was just a baby. I didn't have time to deal with Dad. Chance was in the Army. Colt was at a point where he could either reenlist or get out. Most men would have let a father that bad rot, but not Colt. Even in the Army he'd always been the one to jump in and save the day. He's highly decorated. Did you know that?"

Somehow, Natalie wasn't surprised.

"He's the most heroic man I know, but inside he's deeply damaged," Claire said sadly.

Natalie felt as if she were inside a snow globe, one that'd been shaken and then flipped right side up. The snow in front of her faded away and she suddenly understood. She knew why Colt was so standoffish. Why he closed himself off from the world. Why he didn't want to get too close to people.

"My Lord," she heard herself say.

"I think my dad was jealous of Colt from a young age. He knew his son was a better horseman, a better trainer, hell, just a better person. I was terrified of riding, but who wouldn't be when they knew the penalty for forgetting to buckle a bridle. Colt didn't let that get in the way. He kept at it, and if there was a horse my dad couldn't ride, Colt would ride it instead. Drove our dad crazy."

"It made Colt even better."

Claire caught her gaze. "Exactly. It was a double-edged sword. My dad was evil. No doubt about it, but where Hank was brutal and unfeeling, Colt was gentle and soft. Our brother Chance used to say there wasn't a horse in the world Colt couldn't train."

That was why Jillian had told her to go to him. Her friend had known he'd be perfect for her. Did she know about his past, too? Natalie would bet she did.

She didn't realize she'd been staring at Colt until Claire said, "You like him, don't you?"

Her immediate inclination was to deny it, but she didn't. Instead she said, "Of course I do. He's been wonderful to me."

"That's not what I meant and you know it." Claire admonished her with her eyes. "You *like* him like him."

Natalie couldn't deny it. That kiss had changed everything. Although maybe it wasn't that kiss. Maybe it was the time he'd rested a hand on her thigh, the look of approval on his face doing something to her insides. Or the time she'd watched him ride Playboy, so perfectly brilliant with her horse, so amazing to watch. She'd been left breathless. And then afterward, the way he'd touched her. The kiss had been spontaneous, but it'd cemented what she'd known deep down inside. He had a gentle soul.

She was drawn to that soul.

"I really do like him." She glanced at Claire. "Like him a lot."

Colt's sister smiled softly. "Good. He likes you, too. That's why I wanted you to know about his past. I've watched over the years as women have made plays for my brother, but he just puts them off."

"Like Sam."

Claire nodded. "Like Sam, but she's not right for him. She's too…superficial." She must have realized that sounded bad and so she added, "I mean, she wears too much makeup, and always has to have the fancy jeans. Loves attention. I honestly think she wants to date Colt for the wrong reason. She sees him as her ticket to the limelight. Colt might be a rodeo performer, but it's not because he craves fame. He does it for the horses. That and he can make a living at it. Being successful is just the icing on the cake."

"He *is* good at it."

"Yes, he is. He's a good man, too, Natalie. He really is. Unfortunately, he never lets a woman close enough to see that."

Colt must have sensed they were talking about him because he looked up. Natalie smiled and nodded. Colt leaned toward his nephew and said something, but Adam hardly noticed. The next instant he made his way toward her.

"Don't give up on him," Claire said quickly. "He deserves his chance at a happily-ever-after and he'll need a woman like you, someone who refuses to quit, who won't take no for an answer, someone with kindness in her heart."

Natalie felt strangely close to tears. She appreciated Claire's vote of confidence, but she doubted Colt would make it easy. To be honest, she wasn't certain she would ever break through his cool reserve.

But suddenly, she wanted to try.

THEY'D BEEN TALKING about him.

Colt knew it the moment he spotted Claire's guilty

face. His sister had never been any good at hiding her feelings.

"Whatever it is she's told you, it's not true," he said.

He saw surprise on Natalie's face, but then she smiled, a different kind of smile than he was used to seeing. Gentle. Warm. Almost shy.

"Actually, I'm pretty sure it is true." The gentleness turned into a kind of sadness. "Do you have a minute? I wanted to talk to you."

After seeing his nephew bask in the glory of Hawkman and the joy on the faces of all the other sick children who'd gotten to visit with the famous comic-book character, well, Colt almost told Natalie she could have all the minutes she wanted.

"Sure." He could tell she wanted to apologize. And he would accept. More than that, he would make it clear that he understood. "There's a coffee shop inside the cafeteria if you want to go down and grab a cup."

"That sounds great."

Claire waved goodbye. Natalie followed him, but it was hard to exit the room with so many people crammed inside. Little did they know, they'd attracted quite a crowd outside the room, too. Doctors and nurses, even what looked to be a maintenance man, and then Rand Jefferson's PR people, one of whom nodded and waved to Natalie.

Did Natalie know Rand Jefferson? Colt had been trying to puzzle that out. He'd assumed the hospital had arranged the visit with Natalie's help, but every once in a while the star would catch Natalie's eyes and smile in a way that seemed far too personal. He wondered whether they might have been lovers at one time.

He'd hated that thought, and it shocked him how much. Yeah, he and Natalie had kissed, but that'd been a moment of weakness. It wasn't as if he planned a future with her. He'd known for a long time that he'd never get married, never have kids, never have any of that. Relationships were too messy. Look at his parents, and look at what Claire had gone through. Far simpler just to avoid the whole process. Still, he appreciated Natalie's efforts. Whatever was between her and that movie star was her business, not his.

But it still bothered him. Damned if he knew why.

Chapter Thirteen

They took the elevator to the cafeteria level, a huge open area that had Natalie marveling at the way they'd managed to make it look like a food court in a mall.

It smelled like third grade. Natalie paused for a moment and wondered why, smiling when she realized it was the spaghetti and baked bread. Today, though, the scent mixed with coffee. Scattered men, women and children sat at tables decorated with pink balloons that said MOM on them. There were the occasional doctors and nurses, too, but for the most part it was filled with family members. The sight saddened her. So many people; so many moms; so many sick children.

"Over here," Colt said, leading her toward a kiosk that sold brand-name coffee and was surrounded by tables with green patio umbrellas. They took their place in line while Natalie scanned the menu board for her favorite coffee drink.

"Did you hear Rand Jefferson is visiting the oncology ward?"

A young brunette in a bright blue smock leaned toward her companion, another pretty nurse, both of them with their hair pulled back.

"I heard," said her friend. She wore a blinking red light that had been pinned to her lapel. It flashed the word Mom.

"I'm hoping I'll catch a glimpse of him on his way out."

Colt exchanged glances with Natalie. It just blew her mind that they were talking about her long-time friend in such hushed tones. It made her laugh.

She caught Colt staring at her.

"My treat," he said. The look he gave her made her uncomfortable for some reason.

When the two nurses walked away, still gibber-jabbering about Randy, it was their turn to order. Natalie was still trying to figure out what she'd seen in Colt's eyes. She ordered her favorite sugary-sweet drink, one with whipped-cream topping, little candy sprinkles and more calories than a serving of choco-late mousse. Her mouth watered in anticipation.

"Thanks," she said, saluting Colt with her drink. "I needed this."

They took a seat at one of the round tables. It al-ways struck her as silly that the business placed um-brellas indoors. Wasn't like they might get rained on. Not unless the fire sprinklers went off.

"You okay?" she asked.

She hadn't planned to. There was just something about the way he went to staring at his white cup—a plain coffee. He had half-moon circles under his eyes. Eyes that seemed more sad than she'd ever seen them before. Mussed hair. She liked him without his hat, she thought to herself. He had nice hair. She had the urge to run her fingers through it or maybe brush aside a lock that'd fallen over his tan forehead. He had crinkles along the sides of his eyes. The deeper parts were white, a testament to how much time he spent in the sun.

"I'm fine."

No. He wasn't. Sam had told her he'd been burning the candle at both ends. Racing home after a performance, catching a few hours of sleep, then driving south to visit his nephew, only to turn around and head back home so he could take care of chores. He'd rebuffed almost everyone's offers of help. Except on the weekends. He couldn't be in two places at one time, and so they'd all been pitching in to take care of his ranch and his sister's place when he wasn't around. Jillian had tried to tell her to stay away. Natalie hadn't listened. What Colt didn't know, wouldn't hurt him.

"Stop frowning at me," he muttered.

Was she? She took a sip of her coffee before saying, "You need to slow down."

That wasn't what she'd come down here to say. She'd been all set to apologize to him again. To beg his forgiveness. Ask if he'd reconsider helping her, but she was kidding herself. Even if he did want to help her—and she had a feeling nothing had changed about that—he didn't have time to devote to training Playboy. Not like before. His life was in shambles right now and the last thing he needed was for her to put even more pressure on him.

He had ignored her commentary on slowing down, she noticed, as she took another sip of her chocolate coffee. "I mean it, Colt." She set down her drink. "The work you do. Performing with large animals.

Accidents can happen if you're not paying attention. Ask me how I know."

Those gold eyes of his narrowed. "What did you need to talk to me about?"

Stubborn, obstinate man. She'd never met someone who could blow so hot and cold. "Nothing, really. I just wanted to apologize again for what happened."

"How's Playboy?"

And there he went brushing her off again. "He's doing great. I actually cantered him all on my own again."

"Loped."

"Excuse me?"

"Western riders call it a lope."

"Oh, yeah." She smiled. "I sometimes forget."

He lifted his drink to his lips and Natalie followed the motion, transfixed by the way moisture gathered on the lower one, the memory of how he tasted making her look away. Goodness. Her cheeks burned.

"So you're not going to give up riding."

Her chin shot up. "I told you I wouldn't." And she hadn't. She'd found someone else to help her. "I took your advice. I'm trying hippotherapy and it seems to be really helping. Sam is lending me a hand, too."

His lashes had swooped down. His whole body had tensed, too. Clearly, he didn't like that she'd chosen to ride again.

"Let me ask you something," she continued. "If someone told you to give up riding, if they insisted all you ever did was pet horses on the face, and then spend your life training other people to ride them, would you do it?"

He considered her words—she had to give him

props for that. "No." He met her gaze. "Doesn't mean I have to like you doing it, though."

He wasn't really angry with her; he was upset at having to admit he understood. He was too honest to deny it. Her estimation of him rose even more.

"It's okay. I promise to keep my eye up." She could tell he tried to place the comment, and spotted the exact moment when he recalled her riding in his arena and the trouble she'd had until she figured out not to look down.

"Keep it way up," he ordered.

She nodded. "I'm still working with Sam, you know."

His shoulders twitched beneath his tan shirt. "I know."

"And you did such a great job with Playboy I'm thinking it won't be long before I can try riding without a bridle again. Not right away," she quickly added when she saw the look he shot her. "In a little while."

His jaw ticked. She could tell he was trying hard to keep his thoughts to himself. His hand grasped his coffee cup so tightly she thought he might crush it.

"Honestly, Colt, I'll be fine."

He looked away. Both their gazes caught on a little boy being wheeled toward the cafeteria. He was as gaunt and pale as the children she'd seen in news reports from third-world countries. She knew Colt was thinking it, too, wondering if Adam would look like that one day soon.

"Damn it," he said, thrusting his cup down so hard she worried the lid might pop off. "I don't have time for this."

She leaned back as he stood up. "Time for what?"

The question seemed to take him by surprise, almost as if he'd been thinking one thing while saying another. He'd been focused on Adam, about what the future held. She didn't know how she knew that, but she did.

"To help you," he said instead.

"I know."

"You know?"

She took his hand then, gently pulling him back down. He didn't pull away, his warm fingers once again reminding her of that other time. The time in the feed room...

Focus.

She took a deep breath. "Colt, I didn't orchestrate the whole deal with Randy just so you would go back to helping me again." Okay, so maybe it had crossed her mind. Maybe she'd been hoping to replace Sam because no matter how much she liked the woman, as a trainer she was nowhere near the level of Colt. And hippotherapy could only help so much, especially since it didn't involve trotting and loping. "I did it as a way to thank you and to cheer up Adam, because I know how scared the poor kid must be. Remember, I spent months in a hospital, too. And Claire, too. You're all under a tremendous amount of stress and I hope my friend's visit helped you forget that for a minute."

"Your *friend*?"

She almost smiled. "Yes, my friend." Golly, he almost seemed jealous. "I've known Randy for a long time." She quickly repeated everything she'd told Colt's sister, only at the end she said, "I told him I needed a favor. Randy was only too happy to help. He's a nice guy."

He was trying to assess the truth of her words. She could tell by the way his eyes darted over her face, as if looking for a fatal flaw—a nervous tick. A guilty expression in her eyes. Although why he should care was beyond her.

Unless…

"He's always after me to go out on a date with him, but that whole Hollywood lifestyle's not for me."

Bull's-eye. Colt's eyes narrowed. His knuckles around the cup turned white. He didn't like it. Didn't like her talking about another man. Didn't like the idea that she might be romantically interested in him.

Because Colt liked her.

He didn't want to admit it. He'd closed himself off from his emotions for so long he probably wouldn't know his own feelings if they walked up and slapped him in the face.

"Just remember what happened to Jillian if you ever change your mind."

Jillian's long-ago romance with a movie star had left her with a broken heart. "Randy's different. He really cares about kids. One of these days he's going to be a great father."

She didn't know why she egged Colt on, but she was rewarded by the sharp jerk of his arms as he gulped down the last of his coffee. When he slammed the cup back down he said, "Well, if they ever re-make *Robin Hood: Men in Tights*, I'm sure they'll give him a call."

She almost laughed. She didn't know why, but suddenly she felt giddy. Happy. So very, very tickled pink.

"I'll introduce you," she said. "You'll like him."

He didn't say anything, just sat there staring at the people sitting nearby. When he abruptly stood up, it startled her.

"One lesson a week. That's all I can swing."

Wait. A lesson?

"You can bring Playboy by in the evenings. We can feed and water Claire's dogs together afterward."

"You're going to *help* me?"

"Yeah. 'Cause I don't trust Sam not to kill you."

She didn't know what to say. Didn't know what to do. Actually, she did. She stood up, too, slid her arms around him before he could close himself off to her yet again. "Thank you, Colt."

Their gazes connected and she saw the way his pupils constricted and then flared, his nostrils doing the same. The way he softened for a moment before he tried to move away. She wouldn't let him.

"I promise not to kill myself."

Something about her words must have caught his attention because he froze. She thought he might try to pull away again, but then she felt his thumb begin to move. He gently caressed her back.

"That's the point," he said softly. "I'm not going to let you die."

Oh, dear God in heaven. He really did like her. And she liked him, too. It was a moment of revelation, one that took her breath away. For an instant she contemplated reaching up on tiptoe and kissing him again, but she didn't want to push her luck.

Soon.

She'd have to take it slow. Or maybe she'd have to push Colt hard and fast. Or maybe she should leave him out of her life because if she fell off...

No.

She wouldn't think that way. She was ready to live life to the fullest. Lord knew she deserved a break. She didn't know what the future would hold for her and Colt. Would have to play it by ear. All she knew was that Colt Reynolds was the most amazing man she'd ever met.

She wanted to know that man.

Chapter Fourteen

Stupid, ridiculous, son of a—

Days later Colt still couldn't believe he'd agreed to help her again.

Actually, yes, he could. When she'd been talking about Randy, explaining what a "great guy" he was, he'd lost his sanity. *He* was the one who'd been helping her, not Randy. And so he'd volunteered.

He swiped his palms over his face.

Again.

Not far from where he stood the roar of the crowd signaled the end of a barrel-racing run at the Redding rodeo grounds. Though it was evening, it was bright as day thanks to sodium lighting, and still eighty degrees. The crowd cheered again and Teddy pricked his ears forward and glanced back in the direction they'd just come from—the arena. Judging by the decibel level, the rider had finished with a good time, whoever she was. The drone of the announcer's voice was blocked by the stadium-style seating, so Colt glanced toward the stands, hoping to catch a glimpse of the score board…

He did a double take.

There beneath the scoreboard. Natalie. And walk-

ing with her was none other than the star of the big
screen and the DC Comics universe, Hawkman—
sans the wings. Thank goodness.

"There he is," Colt heard Natalie say when she
spotted him, a big smile on her face. "Surprise!"

She showed up hundreds of miles away from home
with a Hollywood star and all she had to say was
surprise?

He didn't like her one-word greeting because what
he wanted her to do... No, what he wanted to do
to *her* was walk up to her and kiss her so hard she
wouldn't be able to breathe.

Lord help him.

"Hey, Colt," Rand said, smiling his Hollywood
grin and waving.

Not for nothing was Rand's face plastered all over
every billboard and magazine cover in the country.
More than a few people gave the star a double take.

"Oh, my God," Colt heard someone say. He stood
on the passenger side of his four-horse trailer, and
there were dozens of other rigs parked around him,
so he couldn't tell who'd spoken. "Is that Rand Jefferson?"

Ah. Mystery solved. A cowgirl dressed in a short
skirt and boots that would never get near a Western
saddle slipped from between the rigs straight ahead.

"It *is* Rand Jefferson," he heard her friend say,
another buckle bunny with an equally silly pair of
boots on her feet. To give them credit, they kept on
walking, but they were gawking so hard they nearly
decapitated themselves on the gooseneck portion of
a six-horse that'd been detached from its ride.

"I think he's in shock," Natalie said as she and

Rand approached on the dirt road that circled the rodeo grounds.

Colt had managed to forget that he hadn't liked seeing Natalie smiling up at the six-foot-six actor. But watching her walk toward him with the blond movie star towering over her in a very masculine way, made Colt grit his teeth.

Yup. No doubt about it. Jealousy had reared its ugly head.

"I'm not in shock," he forced himself to say, as he plastered a smile on his face and thrust a hand out to shake *mano a mano*. "I'm just wondering why he's not wearing his green tights."

The massive man with the light-colored eyes smiled, and it was no wonder he made women swoon, because that grin of his oozed friendliness.

"Please," Rand said. "Don't remind me of those tights. I hate the things."

Yeah, but they matched the color of his eyes, Colt noticed. He released the man's hand, reminding himself he needed to be nice, especially since Rand had put such a huge smile on his nephew's face. The celebrity visit had made Adam the darling of Children's Hospital. He'd still been floating on air when Colt had left his bedside two days ago.

"Natalie tells me you hate the wings, too," Colt remarked.

He didn't like having to look up at a man, though. Didn't like the way Natalie stared up at the man, either. Didn't like the way seeing the two of them standing there together made him feel.

"The strap that holds them itches like the dickens."

"Excuse me…"

They all turned. A young girl stood there. Colt recognized the black shirt and jeans she wore as belonging to the local drill team. "Can I get your autograph?"

"Sure," Rand said, smiling.

From nowhere the girl produced a pen and a piece of paper. Natalie and Colt watched as Rand performed his PR duties. When he'd finished, the girl slipped away with a silly grin on her face.

Colt asked the question that'd been hovering near the edge of his lips since he'd spotted them. "What are you doing here?"

The words hadn't come out sounding exactly sociable-like. Colt took a deep breath wondering how he'd let his feelings slip so completely out of his control. He and Natalie were friends. That was *it*.

"It was Randy's idea," she answered.

He forced himself to smile. "A romantic getaway?" *Damn*. What was *with* him?

"It's not like that." Her eyes were so blue they reminded him of the tail feathers of wild birds, the kind that lived on tropical islands. She wore a simple denim shirt that buttoned part way down and showed a hint of cleavage, large hoop earring and black pants with cowboy boots—and she couldn't have looked sexier if she'd tried. "There's nothing between Randy and me."

Not yet. That's all Colt could think about. The sick feeling in his stomach, the one that had appeared upon admitting to himself he liked Natalie far more than he should, worsened.

"I told him what you did for a living and he seemed fascinated. He's in between films right now, so when he offered to fly us north to watch you perform, I said sure. The upside is we'll fly back tonight."

Fly? "You mean you took a plane?"

Of course they had, stupid idiot. They couldn't exactly ride brooms.

"Sure. A jet, actually," said Rand in his ultra-masculine voice, forcing Colt to look up once again to meet his gaze. Damn, he hated that. Another young fan approached, this one dressed all in black, too. It was like seagulls on a beach. Once one had been fed, it opened the floodgates. Rand deftly signed autograph after autograph, each young girl saying a quick, gushing thank you, then walking away, only to be replaced by another. One by one he signed autographs for the entire drill team. Rand took it in stride, looking up and saying, "The Redding Airport has a jet center. And the crazy thing is we ran into some of the rodeo performers there."

He'd flown her north in his personal jet. Probably had a limo drop them off at the airport back in Santa Barbara. No doubt he'd paid for everything, too. Colt glanced at Natalie, knowing she'd read the unspoken words in his eyes. *Not a romantic getaway, my ass.*

"A lot of PRCA cowboys hire jets." Natalie glared back at Colt and so he knew she'd understood his silent comment. But far from appearing chagrined, she seemed delighted.

"When you're trying to make big money you need to hit as many rodeos as possible. It makes sense to take a jet," she commented.

"Wow." It was Rand who'd spoken. He'd finished signing autographs, the girls all walking off, giggling and clearly delighted with their prizes. "Who knew?"

"Who knew what?"

They were interrupted by another newcomer, who drew up short when she caught sight of the man next to Natalie.

"Oh. My. Gosh." Sam's mouth hung open. "It's Rand Jefferson."

Colt just stared because with each word Sam's voice had risen half an octave. The *Jefferson* had come out sounding like a squeak. And then she screamed, so loudly Teddy jerked his head up and spun to face her.

"Easy there," Colt soothed his horse, walking toward where he was tied near the end of the trailer. "It's okay." He rested a hand on Teddy's taut neck.

When he glanced back at his long-time friend, she was bouncing from foot to foot, looking ridiculous, especially given her attire. She'd changed out of the red spandex bodysuit that she used for performing and wore what Colt liked to call her *Toy Story* Jessie outfit. Oversize red cowboy hat with white lacing and a stampede string that dangled down the sides of her face. Long-sleeved white shirt with red piping above the pocket. She'd even done her hair in pigtails, except hers were black. She'd told him it was a fashion statement. Colt wasn't so sure.

"Calm down," Natalie said with a laugh. "You're upsetting Teddy."

"Easy there, horsey," Rand said.

Okay, bonus points to Rand for caring about his horse. Minus points for calling Teddy a horsey.

"He'll be okay," Colt said. "Just as soon as Sam *knocks it off.*"

Sam got the message. Colt shook his head, catching a glimpse of Natalie's face. She was laughing inside. Howling, actually.

"I'm just such a huge fan." Sam came forward and clutched Rand's hand as if he were Jesus come to take away her sins. "I've seen *all* your movies."

That would be impressive, Colt thought, if there'd been more than *one*.

"When you played that waiter in *Aftershock*, I just knew you'd be a big star."

Natalie and Colt exchanged glances. *Aftershock*? What the hell movie was that?"

Natalie just shook her head before asking, "You've seen *Aftershock*? Wow. I'm impressed."

"She's the *only* one," Rand said, trying to disentangle his hand. Sam wouldn't let him go.

"You were great." Sam's voice was full of reverence. "When you said, 'Can I take your plate,' you used just the right amount of sarcasm."

Stalker Sam. It'd be Colt's new nickname for his friend.

"Wait a second." Rand's voice had gone from nervous to curious. "Didn't you ride with Colt today?"

"I did." Sam bounced up and down on her toes. "Of course, my portion of the act wasn't half as exciting as it's going to be once Natalie teaches Roger how to jump." She took a deep breath, straightened her shoulders and let go of Rand's hand. "I'm Samantha and I'm part of the Galloping Girlz, except my girls aren't here today. We, Colt and I, were just trying a portion of our new act on for size. The girls and I will be joining him next week." Sam's face lost its enthusiasm. "That is, unless he's needed back at home. You know. For other things."

The other things being Adam and his illness. As a dampener, it worked like a charm. Sam stared down at her toes.

"How is Adam?" Rand asked.

Colt didn't want to like the man. He really didn't, but it was hard when he so clearly cared. Colt had convinced himself the actor had arrived at Adam's bedside as part of a publicity stunt, no matter that Natalie told him otherwise. He realized in that moment, though, that Rand's visit had come from the heart. Just as Natalie had said.

"He's doing okay, but the chemo's really starting to hit him hard." Colt took a big swallow of his own pride. "Your visit really helped his spirits."

Rand's eyes had grown sad. "Let me know when I can come by again. I'd like to keep track of his progress."

Nice guy. No denying it. "I'll do that," Colt agreed.

"Wait." Sam crossed her arms and Colt was glad to see she'd regained some of her self-respect. "Rand visited Adam in the hospital?"

"We're old friends," Natalie explained. "I asked Randy if he'd mind dropping by."

"And he did?" Sam asked.

"A couple of days ago," Natalie said. "And before you ask, I didn't mention it to you because we haven't worked together since then. Plus, I didn't know you were such a huge fan."

"And you didn't tell me?" Sam said, turning to Colt with a look of insulted dignity. "You know how much I love this man."

He did? "Given the way you just reacted I'm glad

I didn't tell you. You probably would have caused a wreck while I was driving."

Sam had the grace to look abashed. "I know." She smiled up at Rand. "I'm sorry for acting like such an idiot."

She still wore her performance makeup and on some women it might have been too much, but on Sam it looked good. Colt could tell Rand thought so, too.

"That's okay," the actor said gently. "Call me Randy. And you can make it up to me by introducing me to your horse. It was amazing the way you hung upside down on him out there in the arena."

Sam's face lit up. "Sure. *Randy.*"

And off they went. Sam didn't even say goodbye. Rand didn't, either.

"A match made in heaven," Natalie observed.

Colt couldn't hide his surprise. "You think?"

Natalie nodded. "They both crave the spotlight. They both look like they were sculpted by a doll maker at Mattel. They both think of physical fitness as a religion. Perfect."

She meant it. He could see that. And she didn't care. Any lingering thoughts that Natalie might have the hots for her friend disappeared when Colt spotted her sunny smile.

"To tell you the truth it was part of the reason I agreed to come today," Natalie confessed, her smile growing. "I've been wanting to introduce the two of them, I just wasn't sure how to approach it. Of course, Sam nearly blew it there at the beginning. I had no idea she was such a huge fan."

"Neither did I."

They looked at each other and laughed and it was the first time he'd laughed in, well, in a long, long while. Weeks, in fact. It felt good. It felt…right.

"I'm sorry to surprise you like this."

He had to look away lest she see how completely *not* a problem it was. "No. It's okay."

And it was. He'd missed her while they had been on the outs. Missed her and thought of what it'd been like to kiss her, and wondered what he'd do if he had the opportunity to kiss her again. He couldn't believe how badly he wanted to do that.

"I have to put Teddy away." He unclipped his horse. "The pens are over here. Walk with me?"

Natalie followed as he headed to the back of the rodeo grounds. The crowd roared. Colt figured they must be just about done with barrel racing by now. "Couldn't be a better night for a rodeo."

The weather. Great. Could he sound any more shallow?

"I know. I brought a jacket, but once we landed I realized I didn't need it."

They passed a group of bull riders heading to the announcer's stand on the far side of the rodeo grounds. Must be the ones Rand and Natalie had met on the way in.

"Are they riding tonight?" she asked.

"Nah. They're probably in slack or in the main performance tomorrow. But I bet they rode earlier."

Above them insects buzzed around the lights. The crowd cheered again. A helicopter droned in the distance. Typical sounds of a late-night rodeo, yet it all felt different with Natalie by his side.

"You mean they've already competed today? As in somewhere else?"

He patted Teddy's neck as he walked alongside her. "Probably flew in from out of state. Happens all the time. Especially when a lot of money is on the line. The Redding Rodeo is one of the richest in the nation."

They'd reached the pen he used for Teddy. The horse was quietly standing in a corner, seemingly oblivious to the cowboy that rode by, the sound of livestock in the distance and the regular cries of the crowd. They must be on bull riding by now, judging by the sound of the bulls braying their displeasure.

"Throw him a flake of that hay there, would you?"

Natalie did as he asked. He tried not to notice how the jeans she wore hugged her bottom. It was that kiss. That damn kiss they'd shared. It had changed everything, left him wanting more, left him wanting *her*.

"You know, I bought Playboy not far from here," she said as she threw the hay.

"Yeah?"

"Right down the freeway, in Red Bluff."

That's right. Jillian had told him. She'd bought him at a famous local auction, the Red Bluff Bull and Gelding Sale.

"Speaking of Playboy, I have a question for you." He turned to face her, resting an arm on the top rail of the pipe panel. "I thought you might want to ride him in a competition in a couple months."

"Excuse me?"

She clearly hadn't understood him, or maybe she hadn't heard him properly. He went on, "It's nothing big, just a local reining show. I thought it might help for you to have a goal."

"You're kidding."

Her blue eyes went wide. She was like a deer that sensed something in the woods.

"You'll do fine."

"You mean you actually *want* me to ride?"

"Of course."

"But I'm not ready."

"Not now, but you will be."

She clearly didn't think so.

"It's okay." He had to resist the urge to reach out and touch her. "We have some time. And when the event rolls around, I'll be there with you."

Her eyes scanned his, first one and then the other. "But the other reason I came here tonight was to tell you face to face..." He saw her take a deep breath. "I've decided to do things your way. I'm going to train horses full time. From the ground. No more riding. Not now, at least, and maybe not ever."

He couldn't have been more shocked if she'd told him she'd decided to run for president.

"Don't look at me like that." She lifted her chin. "I'm okay with it. Really."

He didn't know what to say. He'd never had someone, especially a female someone, consider his opinion and then make such a life-changing choice based on his words. It made his world shift. Made him feel off balance. Made him want to pull her toward him... again.

She added, "I was hoping you'd want to keep riding Playboy, you know, until I'm back on my feet. Provided you have time, of course."

Why was he so poleaxed? "Of course."

It was the relief, he admitted. He wanted to pull her to him and kiss her senseless and tell her she'd made the right decision. Except he couldn't. They didn't have a relationship like that. It was for that reason, and that reason only, that he said what he really didn't want to say.

"I think you should keep riding." The words stuck in his throat, but he spat them out anyway. "I don't think you should give up."

Her mouth opened, but she didn't seem to know what to say. Whatever words she might have formed were interrupted by the sound of her cellphone chiming. It wasn't a call, though. A text, Colt realized when she glanced at the screen, pressed a button and then read.

"You're not going to believe this," she said.

When she met his gaze again, he could see surprise mixed with amusement and something else.

"I've been ditched."

"Ditched?"

She nodded, a smile alighting on her face. "By Randy." She tucked her phone back into her pocket. "It looks like my friend has taken a shining to your friend. They're driving up to Lake Shasta and apparently we're not invited."

Chapter Fifteen

She couldn't believe it. Actually, she could. Natalie'd had a feeling about Sam and Randy. He might be a big-time actor now, but she knew the kind of women he liked, and Sam was right up his alley. Gorgeous. Outgoing. Just a little bit crazy. Okay, maybe a lot crazy hanging off the side of a horse the way she did.

"So you're just supposed to wait here for them to return?" Colt asked.

"Yup."

Sometime while they'd been talking the rodeo had ended, but the arena lights were still on, illuminating the edge of the river near where Colt's trailer sat. He'd parked along a road near the south shore of the Sacramento River that bordered one side of the rodeo grounds. It was the same spot he always chose when he came to this particular venue, he'd told her, explaining how he could tie his horses to one side of his living quarters trailer and then set up camp on the other. It gave him a view of the river and privacy. He'd set up some chairs beneath a pull-out awning. Natalie had to admit—it was quite a view. If she didn't know better she'd swear they were in the middle of nowhere instead of deep in the heart of a city.

"Has he done this to you before?"

She thought back through her friendship with Randy. "We've always been friends, but we've never hung out like that. You know. We'd see each other at parties when we were younger. Then go to the movies when we were older. When he moved to Hollywood he would call. We'd have coffee every once in a while, maybe go to dinner, but that's it."

They were sitting on the folding chairs. Colt had offered her a beer and she'd accepted. It was the fruity, tangy kind of beer and she loved its lemony taste. No plain malt liquor for him.

"Rude," she heard him mutter.

Yeah. Kind of. Maybe. On the flight north she'd confessed everything to Randy. She'd surprised herself because she'd never been the type to share her deep dark feelings with members of the opposite sex, but Randy had been kind, had encouraged her to make a play for Colt. As she sucked down a sip of beer she wondered if she should, if maybe this was Randy's way of helping things along.

Colt, however, seemed perturbed "Did they say when they'd be back?"

"It's the weekend. I don't think either of us had any plans."

"I'm going to call Sam again."

He'd tried that earlier with no results. The same thing happened now. She watched him tuck the phone back in his pocket with an oath of frustration.

"If I didn't know better I'd think you were mad about having to spend time with me."

His looked up at her sharply. "That's not it."

The unspoken question hung in the air. *Then what is it?* Why was he so riled up?

"I just think it's wrong for him to abandon you like this."

She set down her beer on the cooler that he'd used as a coffee table and said, "Colt, if you're thinking I'm upset because Randy went off with another woman, I told you earlier, there's nothing like that between us"

He *had* been thinking that. She could tell. He might be wearing his cowboy hat, and it might be darker on this side of the trailer than the other, but the ambient light from inside the living quarters cast a glow over his face, and she could tell he was angry.

"You want to know how much of an item we're *not*?" She got up from her chair. "He told me I should jump you."

She saw him straighten sharply. The sip of beer he'd just taken got caught in his throat and he coughed to clear it out.

"At the time I thought he meant in the future, but I'm thinking he meant tonight."

"Natalie—"

"No." She leaned down and rested a finger against his warm lips. "Don't say anything." She replaced her finger with her lips, but only for a second. "You'll ruin it."

He opened his mouth, ostensibly to say the opposite, but she cut him off by plunking herself down on his lap. For a split second he resisted, but then he pulled her to him and she realized she'd gotten it all wrong. It wasn't that he didn't want her. He'd been fighting himself over wanting her too much. His mouth opened beneath hers, the taste of him both bitter and sweet—like the beer they'd been drinking. His arms wrapped around her, pulling her even closer, leaning her over his arm and kissing her in a way that made everything inside her leap to life.

Dear Lord.

She'd known it would be good when he finally let himself go, but even she'd underestimated just how good. He growled deep in his throat and she knew she'd won. When they came up for air, they were both gasping. He shifted. She slipped off his lap and gently pulled him up out of his chair.

He stood still, resisting. She reached up on tiptoe and kissed the side of his neck. She could feel his pulse beneath her lips, and when she opened them, tasted him. Salt and sweet.

He groaned.

She traced a path to his ear with her tongue. He jerked her toward his trailer.

He'd left a light on near the leather couch on the opposite wall from where they stood, and she headed right toward the bed. She took his hand and led him there because he still seemed torn. She refused to give up, and began to undress near the foot of the bed, Colt watching. Her shirt came off easily until the hem got on caught her hair. She flicked her head, trying to get it out of her eyes, causing a dizzy spell that made her reach out and steady herself. She slipped off her boots next, then her jeans, her movements growing more hurried because she fretted that with every passing second he might change his mind. When it came time to remove her underwear and bra, however, she hesitated.

His eyes had gone dark beneath his cowboy hat.

Goosebumps formed along her skin, but not from cold, from excitement. She liked having him watch her. For the first time in her life she was grateful that she liked to wear pretty underwear, in this case matching maroon panties and a bra. She hooked a finger though the lace edge of her panties and slowly began to tug them off.

He didn't move, but it didn't matter because she could sense the tension in him. His gaze became liquid fire as he watched her drag the silk down her legs. By the time she finished, her own sexual tension had escalated to the point where her hands shook.

She slipped her shoulder straps off, her gaze never leaving his, first one, then the other. Her fingers grazed her breasts as she slid down the fabric. Her whole body quickened from the touch, nipples growing hard, though from the pressure of him watching her or from her own excitement she didn't know. One breast sprang free and then the other and she saw him curl his fingers into fists as she unhooked her bra.

"Come here, Colt."

He didn't move, but she had never been more sexually aroused in her life, just from his stare. She knew he felt it, too, just as she knew that deep inside he waged a war, a battle to maintain his distance, to keep her at arm's length. It was safer that way for him.

She closed the distance between them. Heat radiated off his body like a piece of metal warmed by the sun. She placed a hand against his middle.

He gasped.

One minute she stood, the next she was down on the bed, and he was covering her and kissing her and she gasped in shock and then pleasure.

Oh, dear heaven.

He lay on top of her, his tongue slipping into her mouth in the same way she wanted him to slip inside her. Her body jerked. She kissed him back. Ran her tongue along his lips, wrapped her legs around his hips, thrust her own hips upward.

He moved. A single swipe of his thighs against her own, and it nearly undid her. Pleasure burst through her center. She moved, too, and he reciprocated as he went on kissing her. Somewhere along the way he'd lost his hat. She'd lost her mind. He kept moving against her, kissing her, and she knew if he didn't stop she'd find her release. She didn't want that yet. She wanted him.

Her hands found the buttons of his shirt.

"No."

She froze. No?

Her fingers clasped a button. He reared back. His eyes had gone hard. "I said no."

He has scars. Physical and emotional ones.

She heard Claire's voice in her mind and knew why he didn't want Natalie to see him. It made her eyes fill with tears, made her lift a hand to the side of his face.

I love him.

No, she told herself. She couldn't. She didn't know him well enough. But as she stared into his eyes, something inside her shifted and then lurched, tumbling and falling. For a moment she grew dizzy. Poor man. Poor, dear, kind-hearted, damaged man.

"Okay," she said softly, her hand sliding behind his neck and drawing him down again.

He'd withdrawn into himself again. She had to nip his lips to bring him back and then he began to move again. She let him. This time she gave herself to the pleasure until just before her climax. Then her hands moved to the waistband of his jeans.

He froze. She rested a hand against the side of his cheek. He dropped his head to her shoulder.

"It's been a long time," he admitted.

"I know."

He drew back, looked into her eyes. "There are things in my past."

Her thumb moved back and forth on his cheek, enjoying the feel of his razor stubble. "Can't we forget about the past tonight? Can't we both just enjoy each other? Maybe deal with the rest of it later?"

He held her gaze and she saw so many emotions flit through his eyes—desire, sadness, confusion, maybe even…hope.

She clung to that hope, reached up and kissed him again. She felt him move, felt his hand slip between her legs and she knew she was lost. He kissed her again and she felt him down there and couldn't hold back. The first wave of pleasure struck so hard she gasped. The second wave hit and she cried out. The third thrust her over the edge until all she saw were stars.

He held her. Her breathing returned to normal. Somehow he'd shifted her so that she laid half on top of him, although she couldn't recall him doing it. She could feel his heart beating beneath her ear, so proud and strong.

"How long has it been?" she asked.

"Long enough."

"Is it because of the scars? Do you not want me to see them?" She leaned back to search his face. His eyes had widened a bit at the mention of the scars, but he didn't seem upset.

"No," he said. "It's not that."

He must have spotted her confusion because he shifted away from her. She found herself sitting next to him. She grabbed a blanket and covered herself with it. She'd grown cold.

"Your childhood couldn't have been easy," she heard herself say.

"My childhood was nothing compared to what I saw overseas." His brown gaze had turned troubled. "I stopped feeling sorry for myself when I saw what other kids went through over there."

"Oh, Colt." She laid a hand on his thigh. That was the hidden pain in his eyes. It didn't come from his abusive father or the loss of his brother-in-law. It came from seeing things no one should have to see. "You're the most remarkable man I've ever met."

The final piece of her heart slipped away and became his. She reached up, kissed him again. He resisted, but only for a second, then pulled her toward him.

Her cellphone rang. She ignored it.

His mouth opened, their tongues entwined. She began to unbutton his shirt and this time, he let her, thank you, Lord, he let her. Her stupid phone finally stopped, but just as quickly started back up. She didn't care. She felt buoyed with confidence, with a deep-rooted knowledge that this was meant to be. Her rodeo hero would finally be hers.

The phone went quiet, then began to ring again.

They both froze. With an oath of frustration, Colt

moved her away from him, reached for her jeans and pulled the phone from her pocket.

"It's Randy," he said after glancing at the screen.

So it was. She bit back her own oath. "Hey, Randy."

There was a pause, and then the sound of Randy's clearly amused voice as he said, "Just so you know, Sam and I got back a little while ago. I sent you a text, but you never responded, and from the sound of things in there, I know why."

She never knew cheeks could burn so instantly. "What is it?" Colt asked.

She hung up the phone and tried to hide her embarrassment, but she would bet Colt saw it anyway.

"They're outside."

Chapter Sixteen

Natalie got dressed quickly, quietly, Colt watching her the entire time. Though there was only the one light on, he could still see the stain of red on her cheeks, knew by the way she kept glancing toward the door that she'd become hyperaware of the two people on the other side.

They had nothing to be ashamed of. He might have been about to break every rule he'd ever imposed upon himself, but nothing had happened. Nothing, big, anyway. There would be no little Colts running around. Not now. Not ever.

You're the most remarkable man I've ever met.

She'd almost sunk him with those words. Almost. That and the look in her eyes. If Randy hadn't called...

When she finished putting herself back together, she straightened. "I guess we're leaving."

He should have felt relief. Should have done what he always did in these situations: given her a kiss on the lips and sent her on her way. But her words, they'd changed everything.

"I'll walk you out."

She stopped him when he neared the door. "Once,

you told me not to be afraid." She smiled softly. "I'm telling you the same thing."

"What do you mean?"

"You're afraid of falling in love."

He drew back, shook his head. "No, I'm not." He just didn't want to. There was a difference, although she made it damn hard to stick to his guns.

She wouldn't look away. "Aren't you?"

He wasn't. He just wasn't the relationship type. He nearly told her those exact words, but she chose that moment to make her exit. He wanted to hang back inside, but he supposed that would be rude. He caught a glimpse of Sam on his way out. She smiled at him, and it was an amused grin, one that conveyed her glee. Whether it was from spending time with her big-screen idol or at catching him with Natalie, he wasn't sure. Probably the former.

"Colt," she said, "Randy wants to take me home with him tonight. He's promised to bring me back for tomorrow's performance. Do you mind taking care of Roger for me?"

What could he say but, "Sure."

Her smile grew blinding. He glanced at Randy, silently warning him that he better not play games with his long-time friend. The man never looked away. He didn't smile, but Colt saw from his expression and knew his message had been received.

"I can't wait to ride on a private jet."

"It's no big deal." Natalie looked back at him once before turning to Sam. "Like riding on a commercial jet, only more comfortable."

"You stole my line," Randy said.

"And discovered it was true."

All three of them faced Colt this time. "We'll see you back at home," Sam said.

He nodded, but his gaze fell on Natalie and there it stayed until she turned and walked away.

You're the most remarkable man I've ever met.

She didn't mean it. She'd been in the throes of passion. That was all.

But the look that had been in her eyes gave him pause. The softness of her touch. The compassion in her voice: *I know about the scars.*

Who had told her? His sister?

It was one of the first questions he asked Claire when he returned home that Monday. He'd caught her at Adam's bedside. He had driven twelve hours to get home, unloaded Teddy and Roger, unhooked his trailer and driven two more hours to visit his nephew—only to find him sleeping.

"Let's talk outside," his sister said, glancing down at Adam. The boy's pale skin nearly matched the sheet pulled up to his face. He'd been sick. A lot. They'd adjusted his meds and put him on something to help the nausea, Claire had said, but it hadn't helped. They'd done all they could. Sometimes the treatment was worse than the disease.

Colt expected his sister to talk to him outside his nephew's room, but she headed first for the nurse's station, checking out with them in a hushed tone, and then for the elevator. Small talk didn't seem to be her thing this evening, because she kept quiet as they descended to the main floor. She didn't turn toward the cafeteria, either. Instead she headed for the main exit.

"Where are we going?" he asked as they stepped into LA's cool night air. Around them the sound of traffic strummed a steady bass beat. Such a stark contrast to where they lived. In the country it was black as pitch at night. In the city a dull glow cast a pall over everything. Above them the twinkle of airplanes and helicopters competed with the stars. Around them the smell of humanity—car exhaust, fast food and just a hint of garbage—filled the air. You either loved it or you hated it, and Colt had never liked it much.

"Claire, where are we going?" he repeated.

"For a walk."

"To where?"

She motioned with her chin. "A park I found." She wore a blue sweater and jeans and so she shouldn't need a jacket, but she crossed her arms in front of her almost as if she needed to ward off a chill. "It's a little bit of a hike, but it's good to get out."

He glanced around them, seeing nothing but concrete and asphalt and moving vehicles. "Aren't you worried about getting mugged or something?"

She glanced up at him and smiled. "That's such a Colt thing to say."

He paused for a moment. "What do you mean?"

She kept walking and he took a few quick steps to catch up. She waited until he was beside her before saying, "You're so protective."

"I am not."

"You have been since we were little. I've often wondered if it's because we lost Mom so young. And because of…"

"Dad."

He finished the sentence for her, but the image of his brown-haired father was one he banished from his mind. He preferred to think about their mother.

He had a brief image of long black hair pulled back into a ponytail.

"I don't think about Mom much." He hated admitting it. There were times when guilt churned his gut because she'd pop into his mind and he'd remember once upon a time he'd had a mother he'd loved, and she'd loved him, too. The purest kind of love, the love like he'd seen in Natalie's—

He shut down that thought, too. She didn't love him. She didn't know him well enough.

"I do." Claire said. In the distance sirens blared. "I think about her all the time."

"You look like her."

Claire smiled softly. "That's a compliment, but I don't want to talk about me or Mom or the man on the moon. I want to talk about *you*."

He tensed. Waited. She remained quiet, though. It wasn't until they crossed busy streets, passed between more buildings, climbed a small hill, and finally, what seemed an eternity later, entered the park she'd mentioned that she spoke. Even then she waited until they found a bench situated beneath mature trees lit from beneath by small lights. He realized instantly why she liked it there. It smelled like home. Cut grass. Pollen. Water.

"Sit," she ordered.

He felt ten years old, but he did as asked. When he settled onto the bench he realized he had a perfect view of the Hollywood sign.

"Look at that!"

She nodded. "I know."

"Neat."

"We're not here to talk about some publicity stunt sign."

"Did you know it was originally erected by a developer to draw people to the homes he'd built in the hills?"

"Colt!"

"All right, all right. What about me?"

She half-turned on the bench, and he could see her perfectly despite the lack of streetlamps. "Why are you so afraid all the time?"

"Excuse me?" He wouldn't call facing off against angry insurgents cowardly.

"Please." She lifted a hand. "Hear me out."

He had a feeling he wasn't going to like what she had to say.

"Over the years I've watched you shy away from one good woman after another."

"If this is about Natalie—"

The hand lifted again. Only when he stopped talking did she continue. "This isn't about Natalie. This is about other things. Life-changing things. First it was high school rodeo. You were good at bronc riding, Colt. Way better than Chance. You didn't have to work at it. Yet you gave it all up and joined the Army. You were good there, too. Your commanding officer begged you not to sign your discharge papers, but you insisted you had to come home and help nurse Dad when you knew I had things under control. Now you're sabotaging your relationship with Natalie. Why?"

So this *was* about Natalie.

"She's wonderful, Colt. She and Randy arranged for a doctor friend of theirs to look in on Adam. He suggested some different treatment options, things that have given me hope, yet when I spoke to her today and asked how things were going with you two she said you hadn't returned her calls. "Why?"

He crossed his arms in front of himself. "Are you finished?"

She nodded.

"First of all, I stopped riding broncs because I knew there was no future in it."

"You didn't know that. Not for sure. You were good, Colt. You could have been the best in the world."

That was up for debate, but he wasn't going to argue the point. "Second of all, you did not have things under control with Dad. You had your hands full with Marcus."

"I did," she said with a nod. "But I could have nursed Dad just fine."

"Not at the end."

"No. But between you and Chance I could have managed."

"We didn't want you to manage. I wanted to help."

"So you chose to leave the Army, something you were good at, and take up the gauntlet of Reynolds's Ranch. That's my point. You do things the hard way. It's almost like you sabotage yourself."

"That's not true. I haven't sabotaged my rodeo business."

"That's another thing." She leaned in toward him. "You treat your horses better than you do people."

He leaned back. "So now I'm not a people person, either?"

"Why haven't you called Natalie back?"

He knew the answer to that question, too. He'd had a lucky escape there in Redding. For a moment or two Natalie had made him forget about his vow never to get involved. He hadn't called her because it was easier to let things fade away. After all, nothing had happened. Not anything important, anyway.

Keep telling yourself that, bud.

"You're afraid of her."

His gut reaction was to deny it. To tell Claire she was full of you-know-what, but something made him hold his tongue.

"You gave up bronc riding because you were good at it and you knew if you wanted to be better you'd have to commit to it. You gave up the Army for the same reason. You're giving up on Natalie for the same reason, too."

"Not true." He leaned back. "I haven't given up on her. I told her to ride that dang horse of hers."

"Because you care for her." Claire's hand found his.

"She's a pain in my ass."

"But you love her anyway."

That prompted a laugh. "Hardly."

"You were about ready to launch yourself at that actor guy when you caught him staring at her."

"Actors are players." He almost told her about Randy and Sam, but his friend was a big girl and it was nice to have her off his back. Claire would only try and throw a wrench in that.

"Remember how you felt when she told you the extent of her injuries? You about lost your mind."

"Not true."

"And now she's giving it all up…for you."

"Not for me." Okay, maybe he had told her to do exactly that, but in the end it was her choice.

"She loves you. Probably figures if she does what you ask, you'll come around. But she doesn't know you like I do. She doesn't know when it comes to humans, you're a quitter. You'll walk away from her just like you walked away from Chance and me."

"Claire, no." He touched her arm. "I never walked away from you."

"Yes, you did, Colt. You left and you never looked back. But the funny thing is you were there for the man who messed you up. Ask yourself why."

He got up. "Adam's probably awake by now, and it's going to take us fifteen minutes to walk back."

She reached for his hand. "Deep down inside, Colt, way deep down, you bury your love. You pretend it's not there. You walk away from it sometimes, but you can't escape it, not when it really counts."

"I'm heading back."

But his sister made him realize one thing. There was no reason to keep training Playboy. No reason at all.

Chapter Seventeen

He sent her horse back.

Natalie watched Sam unload Playboy with disappointment breaking her heart.

"He said to tell you Redding was fun," Sam said.

Fun? Leaving her breathless with passion. Listening to her spill her heart out. Opening up to her and then never calling her even though she'd left ten thousand messages. *That was fun?*

"And that he respects your decision not to ride." Sam was all smiles as she unloaded Playboy at Via Del Caballo Stables and then placed the lead rope into Natalie's hand. "I hope you're not giving up training though." The smile slipped a little. "You're really good at teaching people how to jump. Roger's a new horse."

Natalie stared at the dark green rope, fighting back tears. She hadn't expected this of him. For some reason she'd thought…

She shook her head. It didn't matter what she thought. This was a signal. A sign that he didn't want her to ignore. Thanks, but no thanks. He didn't want her in his life. At all. And that hurt, damn it.

"No. I'm not quitting. In fact I picked up a few

of my old clients this week. I might even hit up one of the Southern California shows later this month."

"That's great." Natalie could tell Sam was genuinely happy for her. "You're wasting your time here." Her gaze caught on Laney who always seemed nearby. Today she was mucking out someone else's stall. "Well, except for that one. She's a good kid."

Don't cry. Swallow back your disappointment. Don't let Sam see how much it stings to have Colt give back Playboy.

Natalie cleared her throat. "I think I found a horse for her to ride. It's a free lease. One of my old students went off to college, and her parents want to keep the horse. When they heard I was back training again, they asked if I knew anyone who might want to ride their gelding, maybe even show."

"Wow. That's fantastic." Sam headed back to the trailer. Roger was still inside. She unclipped the divider and swung the gelding around. "Lucky girl."

"Very."

Laney was over the moon, but she didn't want to give up on her own horse. Natalie had to give the girl credit. So many kids would have tossed their old horses away. Laney would never do that. She reminded Natalie so much of herself when she'd been younger. Her eyes warmed yet again.

Man, her emotions were really close to the surface today.

He'd sent Playboy back.

Fine. It made her want to call him up. Again. It made her want to drive over to Reynolds's Ranch and give him a piece of her mind.

"You think maybe we can jump Roger through fire today?" Sam asked.

She'd like to set Colt on fire. You didn't kiss a woman, make her cry out in passion, rock her world and make her think there was hope for more, and then never call her back.

"Actually, I was about to tell you we're just about ready," Natalie replied. "This week for sure."

Sam did her little happy dance thing. "Awesome." Roger didn't seem concerned, just watched his owner with pricked ears. "Randy's coming to see me ride this weekend and I was hoping to impress him."

They'd hit it off. Randy had called Natalie and filled her in on all the details. They'd been inseparable since they'd met. Randy had confessed to Natalie that she'd been right. He'd needed someone like Sam. Someone who understood the limelight. Someone who had her own life. She was happy for them. Really.

Don't cry.

She turned toward the arena, ostensibly to set up for Sam, but really so Colt's friend wouldn't see her lose her cool. Stupid. Colt was a fool. He didn't know a good thing when he saw it.

She tried calling him over the course of the next week, Lord knew why. When he didn't answer, she left him a message thanking him for his hard work with Playboy. She didn't expect him to call her back, and when he didn't, she told herself not to take it personally. She'd arrived at a decision. She wouldn't let him shut her out. They still had mutual friends. They would still see each other. She would make sure of that.

She finally let Sam jump through a flaming hoop

two weeks after she last saw Colt. Laney cheered from the rail. It'd made Natalie smile for the first time in days, and when Sam rode over and insisted she come watch her perform that weekend, Natalie couldn't tell her no.

She'd see Colt.

She'd play it cool. Act as though his rejection of her hadn't ripped the stuffing from her self-esteem. With any luck it would throw him for a loop. Maybe shake him up a bit.

SHE REMAINED DETERMINED to act unfazed right until the moment she arrived.

He stood with a woman.

Natalie had come around the edge of Sam's long trailer in the exhibitor parking lot of the Los Robles Rodeo Grounds, which was packed with trailers, horses and their owners. Colt and Sam had parked their rigs side by side so that they had their own little area. Natalie had a perfect view of Colt leaning his arm against his trailer, a cute blonde laughing up at him.

"It's nobody," Sam said, having spotted her standing there even though Natalie didn't see her approach. "Just some local buckle bunny that's been hanging around."

Colt looked up, his eyes beneath his black cowboy hat seeming to look right through Natalie even though he nodded a greeting. She swallowed back her pride and nodded back.

Son of a—

Sam caught her before she could turn away. "Don't."

She never would have figured Sam would end up an ally, but she had.

"Stay. Randy will be here soon and if you want I can ask him to act all gaga over you."

She had never told Sam about her feelings for Colt, but clearly she had guessed. Or maybe the woman had spotted it from the beginning. Lord knew she'd felt kicked in the gut the first time she'd met Colt. The chemistry between them was unmistakable. It was obvious to everyone but him.

"No. Don't do that," Natalie replied. Deep breath. "I'll be all right."

Sam wore her red bodysuit and her oversize red hat with the white lacing. Two months ago Natalie privately might have thought she looked ridiculous, but not today. Today she wanted to hug her.

"You're in love with him, aren't you?" Sam asked.

Ohdeargoodness.

"No." Another deep breath. "I mean, I don't think so."

Liar.

Was she? Not right now. Right now she wanted to kill him. He'd draped himself all over the woman in the tight jeans and low-cut T-shirt. She was laughing up at him and Colt, who almost never smiled, grinned back.

Too hard. "I shouldn't have come," Natalie muttered.

"I wanted you here." Sam touched her arm gently. "We've worked really hard to get Roger to jump through that damn flaming hoop. You're going to watch us perform even if I have to duct tape you to the grandstands."

Dear Sam. She really had grown to love the woman. "Did Colt know I was coming?"

The answer was in Sam's eyes long before it passed through her lips. "No."

Breathe. Just breathe.

But she wanted to crumble. She'd hoped he'd done it on purpose, hooked up with the blonde as a way of making her jealous, that he'd known she was coming and so he'd set the whole thing up. Only he hadn't known. And she...

Wanted to ball her eyes out.

"Chin up, kiddo." Sam smiled. "Remember you've picked up all sorts of new clients. You're a success. Maybe one day you'll ride again and Colt will see you on TV and he'll realize what an ass he was to let you go."

Because clearly he *had* let her go. Clearly he'd moved on. Quickly.

Something warm rippled across her skin. She could feel her cheeks turn red. Anger.

"Good riddance," she said. But she didn't mean it. She knew Colt had a heart. She saw it in the way he handled his horses. It was there in the way he'd touched her. There, too, in his eyes. He just hid it away where it wouldn't get hurt.

"Atta girl," Sam said, even though Natalie spoke about Sam's best friend.

The rest of the day was agony. Randy showed up, nearly unrecognizable in his Wrangler jeans and cowboy boots. He'd let whiskers sprout. The light brown stubble helped conceal his identity nearly as well as his tan cowboy hat. It worked, too, because Colt's new friend, a woman named Christine, had given him a double take, only to ask if they'd met before. Randy had assured her they hadn't and that had been that.

The blonde wouldn't leave Colt's side and that likely had something to do with why she didn't realize she stood next to a celebrity. Too distracted.

When the rodeo started and it came time for Colt and Sam and the Galloping Girlz to perform, Natalie actually had to stand next to Christine, Randy on her other side. It had dawned a bright day. Natalie reassured herself that was why she had to squint her eyes, not because her head had begun to throb, but because it was too bright in the Southern California desert.

"Are you one of the performers?" Christine asked as Colt pulled his rig into the center of the arena. "A barrel racer or something?"

"No," Natalie said. *Be nice.* "I'm a horse trainer."

The woman's pretty blue eyes brightened. "Like Colt?"

Colt's rig had stopped in the middle of the arena, right next to the hoop she and Sam had practiced with for the past few weeks. Behind him, the Galloping Girlz entered, the crowd gasping as one by one they stood on top of their horses.

"Exactly like Colt."

Except I don't ride.

She should, she told herself. What reason now was there to wait? If she fell off, who would care?

Now you're feeling sorry for yourself.

Perhaps she was. Perhaps it was time to brush off her sadness and forget about Colt.

Teddy jumped out of the trailer. Colt lifted his hands and the gelding reared. The crowd roared its approval as around him Sam's friends performed their tricks, Sam at the helm with her long black hair flying. Natalie had to admit, it all left her spellbound. The horses with their manes streaming and their tails held like royal standards, and their hooves pounding the ground so hard they kicked up dirt. The girls hung upside down, off the side or over the rear of their mounts. In the middle of the pen, Teddy appeared sublimely unfazed. He grabbed the scarf from Colt's back pocket and waved it at the crowd who laughed and clapped. Instead of playing tag with Colt, though, the horse fell into line behind the girls.

Natalie had no idea what Colt had trained Teddy to do next. She knew he'd been practicing with the girls. Sam had told her. So she watched as Teddy took off running. He sidled up next to one of the Galloping Girlz, keeping pace with her. Laura, her name was, and she was riding a flashy sorrel with four white socks. She stood. Teddy held his position. Laura slowly stepped off her horse and onto Teddy midgallop, until she was riding him. Bareback. Bridleless. Without a saddle. The crowd cheered and Natalie marveled. How had Colt taught Teddy to do that? Most horses would have run off and done their own thing. Not Teddy. He stayed next to Laura's horse. And all while still holding the scarf.

Despite wanting to hate Colt, Natalie had to admit the act's brilliance. Sam and the girls added a whole new layer and they hadn't even gotten to the best part yet. One by one the girls peeled off. Laura went back to riding her own horse. Teddy skidded to a halt by Colt. They lined up in a row, heads bobbing, nostrils flaring. Only Sam stayed out on the rail, her red outfit a blur against a backdrop of people. In the arena

Colt reentered the trailer. He emerged with a flaming torch. The crowd applauded; they knew what came next. With the flick of a wrist he turned on the propane. The ring lit up with an audible *poof.* This was it. The moment both she and Sam had been practicing for.

Sam guided Roger off the rail.

The flames grew higher. They'd practiced this a dozen times. Still, this wasn't a jump with poles that would collapse. If Sam messed it up Roger could get hurt. They could *both* get hurt and so Natalie's heart lodged in her throat as she mentally counted down the strides between Roger and the jump.

Three.

Two.

One.

They flew. Sam ducked low. The flames danced. They landed on the other side much to the crowd's approval.

"Wow," both Randy and Christine cried. Randy let out a woot as Sam waved to the crowd. Teddy trotted up next to Sam, brandishing his scarf. The girls broke formation and left the arena at a dead run. Teddy followed, but instead of leaving with the other girls, he circled back around, jumping into the back of the trailer and waving his scarf.

"That's incredible." Randy hooted and hollered. "Just incredible."

"You're Rand Jefferson!" Randy and Natalie turned toward Christine, who stared accusingly at the handsome giant. "That's why you seem so familiar."

"Nah." Randy's smile was full of devilry. "I just look like him. I get that a lot."

Christine's mouth went slack. Natalie would have smiled if her heart hadn't still been pounding from watching Sam jump. Somehow, watching her friend perform had brought it all back. The rush of adrenaline as Sam had turned toward the hoop. The concentration it took to time the take off perfectly. That moment of breathlessness as they'd launched, flying, the rider one with the horse.

Damn, she missed it.

Randy caught her eye and his amusement faded. "Good job, coach."

She mustered a smile for his sake. "Thanks."

"You *are* Rand Jefferson," Christine insisted.

Randy shot the blonde an impatient look. "Give us a moment, would you?" He didn't wait for her to respond, just hooked an arm around Natalie's shoulders and guided her away from the rail.

"I don't think you're fooling her anymore," Natalie pointed out.

"Too bad." He frowned over his shoulder. "My friend needs me more."

She faked a groan. "Not another pep talk."

He pretended to twist an imaginary mustache. "Sam asked me to make out with you."

"She did not."

Randy's smile was full of guilt. "Not really, but it's a thought."

She pretended to elbow him, so very grateful for his friendship right then that she really would have kissed him if he wasn't so dang tall. Sam was a lucky girl. Randy might be a big star these days, but he had a big heart, too.

"Sam tells me you quit riding."

She nodded as they ducked between two trailers. "I miss it, though."

"As your friend, possibly your oldest friend." He smiled again. "And the best looking, I might add, I should probably give you a pat on the back and tell you good choice."

She glanced up at him as they walked. "But you're not."

He stopped by the edge of the access road and stared down at her, and for a moment Natalie wondered why she'd never found him attractive. Well, she did, just not in that way. To her Randy would always be the goofy guy who had once laughed so hard his soda had come gushing out his nostrils.

"I'm not," he admitted. "Because I saw the look on your face as Sam jumped through that hoop."

Though she told herself to hold his gaze, she didn't, mostly because the compassion in his eyes nearly undid her.

"Do you remember, once upon a time, when I told you I was going to give up acting?"

The image of a hole-in-the-wall coffee shop came to mind, a place with orange vinyl seats and Formica table tops, and a waitress that'd reminded her of Lucille Ball. "I told you not to do it."

"And do you remember why?"

"Because acting made you happy."

"And…" he prompted.

"Because you had too much talent to throw it all away."

Randy nodded, his hand moving to her jaw. "You, Natalie, are the best rider I have ever seen." He smiled wryly. "Well, aside from Sam. But not even Sam can fly a horse like you do. You're like some kind of mythical being when you jump. I remember watching you at that competition a few years back. The one with that swanky party. You invited me in case I might bump into someone in the business."

"The LA Grand Prix."

"That was it." He snapped his fingers. "You made it to overtime."

"To the jump off," she corrected with a smile.

"Whatever. All I know is there you were, riding into the ring on that beast of a horse that flung its head and tried to take off with you. But you made it behave." He shook his head, his hand still holding her jaw. "It was the most amazing thing I've ever seen, watching you soar over those poles, most of which were taller than you."

She felt her lashes moisten. She remembered, too.

"Don't give that up, Nats. You've got too much talent to throw it all away."

Her smile was full of tears. A few of them fell on to his hand. "What if I fall off?"

"What if you *don't*?"

She let his words sink in thinking all the while that millions of women the world over would give their right ears to have Rand Jefferson gaze down at them like he was at her. Millions of women would never know what a truly amazing guy her friend was.

"I love you, Randy." A platonic love. The love of two old friends. He knew that, though.

"I love you, too, Natalie." He pulled her into his arms. "And if you get into another bad wreck and don't call me when you're in the hospital I will kill you."

She rested her head against his chest. "If I get into another bad wreck you may not *have* to kill me." Her gaze caught on a truck and trailer pulling in. A black truck. One with logos on the front fender. She straightened in Randy's arms. Colt stepped from the truck, and any thought that he might not have seen her faded when he paused, staring in their direction.

She didn't know why she did it. Pride, probably, but she pulled back and looked into Randy's eyes. He'd seen Colt, too, and played his part perfectly as he bent and kissed her lightly on the lips.

Nothing.

America's hunkiest heart throb held his mouth against her own and she felt nothing. Nada. Zip. It was in that moment, that very second, that she admitted the truth.

She loved Colt.

For her there would only ever be one man who made her feel as if she rode on the back of a jumping horse, one that soared over the tallest of obstacles and left her breathless.

She pulled back and smiled. "Thanks."

Her friend smiled back, and they both knew what she needed to do.

Chapter Eighteen

So much for there being nothing between them, Colt thought. He walked around to the back of the trailer. Sam and the girls were congratulating each other as they tied up their horses, still breathless from their performance, their horses' sides streaked with sweat.

"Good job, everyone," Sam called out.

It had been good. Spectacular, really. The crowd had loved it. Colt looked up and met Sam's gaze.

Your boyfriend's kissing his so-called buddy.

Sam smiled. He nodded, turning away. He would never tell Sam what he'd just seen. She was a smart girl. She'd figure out sooner or later the man was playing her. And if Natalie was stupid enough to fall for the actor's big muscles and smooth words, then whatever.

So why does it feel as if you've been kicked in the gut?

He couldn't answer the question. Refused to answer the question. He'd get Teddy all squared away in his trailer and head home.

His cellphone rang.

It was one of those moments when he knew who it was before he checked. His sister.

"Colt," she said. "Adam's really sick."

She didn't need to say another word. "Be right there."

It didn't matter that he was a hundred miles away. Sam must have seen the look on his face.

"What's the matter?"

"I have to get back home."

She must have sensed why. "Unhook your trailer. I'll find someone to hitch it up and drive Teddy home."

"No."

They both turned because it was Natalie who'd spoken. "I'll drive Teddy home. Randy can take you to the hospital."

Randy? "No, thanks."

Natalie rushed up to his side. "Don't be stubborn, Colt. Randy's driving a Porsche. He can fly. Just get in his car and go."

"She's right." Sam came up behind him. "Let Randy take you."

He didn't want to do it. He really didn't, but he knew a good idea when he heard one, never mind that he wanted to sock the guy in the jaw.

"Fine." He tossed his truck keys in Natalie's direction. A quick glance in the actor's direction revealed he was already heading toward his car parked somewhere close by. Colt shoved his cowboy hat farther down on his head and ran to catch up.

"Where are you going?"

Christine, the little blonde he'd been flirting with, stepped in his path.

He didn't want to stop, but common courtesy dictated he make his excuses. "Sorry. I've got to run."

"But…I thought we were going to dinner."

He stepped around her. "Not tonight." He continued under his breath, "Looks like I have a date with Hawkman."

"I knew it!" she cried accusingly from behind him, but Colt didn't stop to figure out what the hell she meant. The only thing he wanted to do was get to Adam's bedside.

Natalie had been right—they flew.

He had to hand it to the movie star. He knew how to drive his fire-engine red Carrera. And he said next to nothing as he navigated the busy Southern California roads. Well, except for once when he'd darted between two cars, cutting it close. Colt's hand dug into the door handle and one of the vehicles honked in outrage.

Even then all Randy said was, "I had plenty of room."

They arrived at the hospital in record time. Colt didn't want to be grateful, not to someone who was clearly playing both of his friends, but he'd never been more relieved.

"Thanks," he said, thrusting open the door.

The actor's eyes were full of compassion. "Tell him Hawkman said he needs to get better."

Colt nodded. "I will."

When he made it to the oncology ward, he was stopped by a nurse. She knew him. Ever since Rand Jefferson's visit Colt had been warmly greeted by the hospital's staff.

"He's not in there."

"Where is he?"

"He's been transferred. I'll take you up, but you can't go in to visit him—"

"What the hell do you mean I can't—"

"Wait, wait." The nurse, one of the pretty little brunettes from the coffee line, held up a hand. "Let me finish. He's what we call immunodeficient. His immune system is compromised and we can't have just anyone walking into his room." Her face filled with empathy. "His mother is in there with him, but she's scrubbed herself down, and she's wearing an antimicrobial suit. You'll have to do the same, and once you go inside there can be no hugging or touching or doing anything that might spread germs."

He nodded. He would have walked through fire for Adam.

The nurse motioned for him to follow her. She asked him a barrage of questions as they entered the intensive-care unit. It took an eternity to climb into the paper-like suit. He felt each passing second like a slow-motion instant replay. When he'd finished, they led him through double doors and into an area filled with glass-walled rooms.

He spotted Adam.

Lying in a bed that looked massive beneath his little frame. Wires were attached to his arms and body, and his hair, once so thick, was thinned out by the cancer-killing drugs they'd pumped into him.

Colt wanted to cry.

Claire looked up at him, her face wet with tears, but Adam was unaware of his arrival. The boy was out cold.

"He has a fever," she said softly, looking so sad and forlorn when Colt entered the room he wanted to rush to her side. They'd warned him not to. It was the hardest thing in the world not to wrap his little sister in his arms—Adam, too—but Colt did as he'd been told. He took a seat on the opposite side of the bed.

"Do they know what's causing it?" he asked.

"They've taken blood. They'll have the results back any moment now, but it could be anything. It could be an infection or a virus—we just don't know."

He nodded. She wiped her tears away with her suited up forearm.

"How did you get here so fast?"

He forced a smile. "Hawkman."

"Rand?"

He nodded. "He was at the rodeo. Gave me a ride back. Natalie is driving Teddy back to the ranch."

"That was nice."

She looked pale, her thick black hair pulled back from her face. Colt's sister was one of those women who would look beautiful no matter what the circumstances, her green eyes made bigger by the white of her bio-suit.

"Thanks for coming." She looked about ready to break down again.

"Are you kidding? Where else would I be?"

They took turns then holding vigil, Claire moving to a chair to get some sleep, then Colt doing the same. Adam floated in and out of consciousness, the fever wracking his body with chills. He woke up screaming at one point, eyes unseeing, hands held out in fear. Fever dream, the nurse called it. Eventually they learned it was a virus that tortured the little boy's body. Nothing they could do, they were told, except give him meds to combat the side effects.

Colt lost track of time, and was catching a cat nap

when someone gently nudged him on the shoulder. It was Claire and she was all smiles.

"The fever broke."

He sat up in the chair. "Are you sure?"

She stepped aside. Adam peered back at him. "Uncle Colt?" His eyes went wide. "When did you get here?"

Once again Colt wanted to cry, this time with tears of relief.

SAM CALLED AND OFFERED TO drive him home, but Colt would hear none of it. Claire took a break first, going back to her temporary lodging near the hospital to shower and rest, and looking much more like herself when she reentered Adam's hospital room.

"How is he?"

"Sleeping," Colt said with a smile.

She nodded. "Your turn."

He took her car, and later on he would look back at that long drive home and wonder how he'd made it. He would have no memory of navigating the roads. His eyes felt like a sand arena and his hands shook from exhaustion, but he made it, his spirits lifting when he drove through the gates of his ranch.

Natalie was there.

She waited for him on his front steps. It was strange because it felt like a month since he'd last seen her. He slowly stepped out of Claire's car.

"I made you some dinner." Natalie stood. "Claire called and said you need to eat, then you're supposed to go straight to bed."

With you?

The thought popped out of nowhere. But, no, he wouldn't give in to that temptation even though he couldn't believe how good it was to see her. Last time they'd been together she'd been kissing Randy. Colt had had time to think about that in the hospital, and upon closer review he knew deep down that it had been a kiss between two friends. Randy had redeemed himself, anyway, sending Adam a get-well basket of candy. He'd had all his A-list actor friends sign the card, the damn thing all Adam could talk about. Between the ride and the treasured gift Colt couldn't stay mad at the guy.

"I'm not sure I can make it up the steps," he admitted.

She smiled, and was that relief he saw in her eyes? Had she worried he'd tell her he didn't need her help? He didn't. Or maybe he did. To be honest, everything seemed muddled, Colt so exhausted it was all he could do to stand.

Natalie had made him steak. He hadn't even realized it was dinnertime. When he'd finished she didn't say a word, just took his plate. He stood, suddenly aware of her there, aware of her placing his plate in the sink, of turning back to him, softness in her eyes.

He wanted her.

It struck him instantly, the need, the want, the desire. He straightened in surprise.

"Bed."

It was all she said, and the single word shot a jolt of responsiveness through him. "Yeah, bed."

But she didn't follow. He paused by his door, wondering, asking himself what he would do if she came into his room. He'd sworn off sex. No. That wasn't true. He'd sworn off having sex with her.

Why was that?

He'd bedded other women. He could have had full-on sex with Natalie, too, but he hadn't wanted that. He hadn't wanted to take a chance.

A chance at what?

His brain went back to being muddled as he stripped down, but he still wondered if she'd show up in his bedroom. He slipped beneath the covers and waited, his hearing hyperattuned to the noises outside his door. Sounded as if she was doing the dishes. Would she slide into bed with him when she was done?

She didn't.

He waited some more, but eventually the waiting gave way to exhaustion. The exhaustion gave way to sleep.

He didn't hear her come in. Never saw her standing over his bed, staring down at him with love in her eyes. Never felt her hands as she reached out to pull up the covers, or saw what happened when she spotted the scars on his back. He didn't see her freeze, didn't see her eyes fill with tears, didn't feel her finger as she touched first one, then the other long line of mutilated flesh, her eyes full of horror and sadness.

He dreamed that she kissed him. His body quickened in response. He wanted her. Had always wanted her. He was just so tired. Tired of fighting. Tired of being afraid.

In his dream she kissed those scars. He smiled because it felt good. It always felt good when she touched him.

He hadn't wanted to risk falling in love. That was the chance he hadn't wanted to take, he admitted to himself in his dream.

"I'm sorry," said his dream-Natalie.

No, he tried to tell her. He was the one who was sorry. He never should have pushed her away like he had. Should have called her and confessed his feelings.

From far away, a voice whispered in his ear, *I love you*.

And he smiled and said, "I love you, too."

And it felt totally right.

Chapter Nineteen

"What do you mean she doesn't keep her horse here anymore?"

Laney stared up at Colt wide-eyed, her mouth dropping open. He told himself to calm down. His words had come out sounding harsh, and he hadn't meant to scare the kid. He'd just been shocked.

"When did she move?" he asked, more gently.

"About a week ago." Laney leaned her rake against a beaten-up fence post, where it cast a long shadow in the late-afternoon sun.

"I'm moving there, too, at the end of the month," the girl continued.

He didn't know what so say except, "Wow."

Laney's chin thrust up and Colt realized she hadn't been surprised by his tone so much as upset and maybe even angry at him for refusing to train her friend. Hell, maybe she even knew he'd been avoiding Natalie.

"Yeah," Laney said. "As soon as she started telling people she was back in business, like, a million people called." She crossed her arms. "They wanted her to be their trainer, you know. At these really fancy places. It's been totally cool."

Hostility. He could see it in the girl's eyes. It made Colt wonder what Natalie had been telling her. "That's great."

She nodded. "I get to ride one of the horses at the new place, too. It's won, like, a million ribbons. I can't wait."

"Good for you."

He was happy for her. Happy for Natalie. Really.

"And you should see the horse Natalie gets to ride. It has to be, like, eighteen hands."

Natalie? Ride? What was this? "I thought she wasn't going to ride anymore."

"She wasn't, but then she changed her mind." She turned, picked up the rake again. "She said jumping was too important to her to give it up."

"She *what*?"

Laney paused, looked back over her shoulder. "She's jumping again."

Her words knocked the stuffing out of him. "She can't be."

Laney nodded. "She said it's actually easier for her to jump horses than it was for her to ride Western. Something about muscle memory." The girl flicked her ponytail over a shoulder. "She still has to close her eyes a lot, but she said that helps with her spots."

"She's seeing *spots*?"

Laney snorted. "A spot is the place where you tell your horse to take off."

His heart had lurched, literally *lurched* when Laney had mentioned spots. It was still pounding as he stood there facing the young girl, because he didn't like the idea of Natalie jumping again. Not at all.

It was that dream, he told himself. That stupid

dream where he'd imagined she'd kissed him and told him she loved him. Ever since he'd woken up he hadn't been able to get that dream off his mind.

"Where is this new place?"

For a moment he thought Laney might not tell him. She twisted the rake around in her hand, the tines peeling off a layer of dirt.

"The other side of town." Laney turned away to resume her work. "The *good* side."

What the hell did that mean? "Does the place have a name?"

"Hawk Hill Farms."

He'd never heard of it, but he would bet Google had. "Thanks."

He was about to get back into his truck when he heard Laney call, "If you're going over there to see her, she's not there."

He paused, hand on the handle. "Where is she?"

Laney's smile was full of pride. "At a jumping competition."

Good thing he'd been leaning against the door because he probably would have fallen otherwise. "Where?"

'Not sure." She went back to shoveling manure. "You'll have to ask Natalie."

SHE IGNORED HIS text messages.

Frankly, she didn't need the distraction of Colt this weekend. She'd sworn Sam to secrecy about her re-entry into the hunter/jumper world—at least as far as Colt was concerned. It'd shocked her how quickly word had spread among her old friends. She'd had three offers to ride former clients' horses, and one of them, a gelding she'd broken to ride herself, had tempted her to try jumping again. He was young and so the fences would be low, but she had to admit to being terrified.

You can do this.

She could. She didn't doubt her ability whatsoever. Well, okay. Maybe a little. The first time she'd flown over a fence she'd had a dizzy spell, but compared to the spins of a reining horse, it was nothing. She'd closed her eyes for a second, regained her equilibrium and ridden on.

"Nervous?" Mariah asked, her red hair its usual frizzy mess.

"Not too bad."

Who was she kidding? She was petrified. What if she fell off? But she was tired of asking herself that question. What if? What if? *What if?*

The world was full of what-ifs.

"Well, if he jumps like you've been practicing, you're a shoe-in."

Natalie had her entire support crew with her. Jillian and Wes. Mariah and Zach. Even Sam and Randy, although the boys had gone off to the bar area. That was the thing about English shows. Very posh. After living in Slumville, it'd been something of a shock to her system to be back amid such luxury. Her new place was no less elegant than the Richfield Hunt Club, where this week's show was being held. It'd been a whirlwind process unearthing her old show clothes and curtains, getting together a list of clients, showings, lessons. Thankfully she'd kept most of the gear she'd known would be hard to replace.

"It's like old times," Jillian said, smiling.

They stood outside the row of stalls reserved for Natalie's customers and their horses. Nestled in the foothills near Los Angeles, the place was new and state of the art. Two years ago Natalie wouldn't have spared any of the amenities a glance. These days she had a fresh appreciation for the white vinyl fencing, the pristine sand footing that looked like powdered sugar, and the old-fashioned-looking barns that were anything but, housing half a dozen arenas—some of them for showing, some of them for warming up. She'd marveled at how a place could look so old and stately, yet be so new, and how much money it must have taken to achieve that effect. Never again would she take such things for granted. Never again would she forget what it was like to be on the other side of that white fence, driving by and wishing she had the money to afford nice things. Business had been good. Less than a month in and already she had half her old clients back. She'd wasted no time trading in her old truck.

"It's good to be here," she said softly.

"Yes, but do you really think you're ready to ride?"

All three of the women turned toward the voice, Jillian letting out a cry of delight. "Colt!"

"Never mind riding. Jumping?"

What started as a warm greeting died a quick and sudden death. Natalie stood there, frozen, a million thoughts flying through her head. What to do? How had he known? Had Sam told him? She hadn't wanted him to find out she'd gone back to jumping horses. Not yet. Maybe not ever.

"Are you implying she shouldn't be doing this?" Jillian said, brushing her short black hair off her face.

"Because if you are, you haven't seen her ride these past few weeks."

Natalie's eyes slipped past him, wondering if rodeo girl was there with him. Carrie or Carol or Christine. Sam had told her she hadn't seen the woman with Colt again, not since that first day, but the memory still stung. He might not have known she was coming that day, but he'd used the opportunity to make her hate him—but the realization didn't make it feel any better. She didn't hate him. After touching his scars that night, dragging her fingers along the physical remnants of his childhood, she could never hate him.

"Can I talk to you?" Colt asked.

He wore his cowboy hat. He might have felt out of place in his jeans and cowboy boots, the belt buckle catching the last waning rays of the sun. In a world of Hermes scarves and Polo shirts, Colt stood out like a jagged rock in a room full of smooth pebbles. He didn't care what anyone thought, though. It was one of the things she loved about him. All he cared about was his family and his horses and maybe his sister's dogs.

Not her.

"Sure," she agreed.

Mariah and Jillian both shot her silent looks meant to question whether she thought that was a good idea. She didn't, but she went with him anyway. "I'll be right back."

Her two friends waved, though she saw them exchange concerned glances before she turned away. Nothing to fear. She was already dressed in her breeches and boots and her long-sleeved cotton shirt—a ratcatcher, they called it, after the rat catchers of old who wore their collars in the same way, tightly pinned around their necks for protection. All she needed to do was slip on her jacket, mount and ride. A few moments with Colt wouldn't hurt, although they might hurt her heart.

He wasted no time. "Why didn't you tell me?"

She shrugged, nodding to one of her long-time friends, a fellow female trainer who eyed Colt like a new pair of high heels she'd like to buy.

"I didn't think it mattered."

He stepped in front of her. She took a deep breath because she knew what was coming next.

"Don't do it," he pleaded.

"You mean ride?" she asked, playing dumb. "Why not?"

She scanned his eyes, hoping to see a speck of... something. Maybe fear for her safety. Or—what she wanted to see more than anything—a need that was even half as urgent as her own.

"This isn't riding around in a Western saddle," he cautioned.

She released a huff of laughter. "You're right. I'm better at this."

Beneath his black hat those eyes she studied so closely grew incredulous. "But you get dizzy."

"I do, but I can find my seat better in an English saddle. Western saddles are too big. I should have gone back to riding English right from the get-go."

"But jumping."

She saw it then. The hint of something she never thought she'd see. Desperation.

"It's no different than riding a horse that's bucking."

His turn to snort. "That's supposed to reassure me?"

The very fact that he needed to be reassured, that she could see the edge of panic now, made her want to weep.

"I'm not trying to qualify for international competition, Colt." She reached for his hand. "It turns out I should have been riding English the whole time. The posting still makes my stomach turn, but once I start to canter I'm fine. Something about being in half-seat. I can keep my upper body from bouncing and it keeps the dizziness at bay."

He clutched her hand. Tightly. Fearfully. Like a man trying to save a loved one from drowning.

Oh, dear heaven.

She couldn't breathe for a second. For about the millionth time since she'd met Colt she found herself on the verge of tears. He cared. He cared a lot.

She had to look away. If he kept staring into her eyes he'd see the joy that blossomed there. Spot the sudden self-doubt because if he cared for her and she did get injured…

No. The days of thinking such negative thoughts were behind her now. It was all or nothing.

For that reason she reached up on tiptoe and kissed him. Hard. "I love you, Colt." Her hand fell to his cheek and she rocked back on her heels. "Wish me luck."

He looked shell-shocked by her words. He blindly gripped her hands, and she could tell he wanted to hold on to her and never let her go. He might not admit it to himself, but she could see it in his eyes.

He took a deep breath, and instead of stopping her,

he did the only thing a man such as Colt could do. He nodded and said, "Keep your eye up."

She bit back a smile. "I will."

Chapter Twenty

He didn't think he could do it. He didn't think he could watch.

"Good luck," Natalie's friends called out as she mounted the gray gelding she was scheduled to ride.

"Remember. He's a little hot at first. But once you warm him up, he'll be fine."

Natalie nodded. The woman who'd spoken was older. The horse's owner, Colt had heard. He'd thought it odd that a woman her age would have such a young and volatile horse, but Jillian had explained that English jumping was a lot like horse racing in that the owners enjoyed watching their animals compete and nothing more.

"I think you need a drink, cowboy," Randy noted as they walked toward the observation tents. Or Rand. Hell. Colt couldn't remember what to call him.

"I'm fine."

"He looks like me when I send a horse off to the starting gate," Zach said, blue eyes full of amusement as he fell into step beside them. His wife, Mariah, smiled and nodded in agreement.

"I'm *fine*," Colt repeated.

Randy and Wes exchanged glances. Colt ignored

them. As a group they headed toward the canvas-covered tents set up between the arenas. The event was called a "mini prix," and it featured some of the sport's outstanding youngsters, or so Colt had learned during the half-hour he'd been forced to watch Natalie warm up the young gelding. She'd jumped him over obstacles that made Sam's flaming ring seem like a Hula Hoop.

The sun had gone down, the lights around the arena throwing long shadows on the ground, the poles so brightly colored they seemed almost neon beneath the fluorescent fixtures. Inside the tent, butane heaters sizzled and hissed. No pre-assigned seating, apparently. They found a table near the rail of the arena where Natalie would ride.

"Here."

Someone pulled out a chair for Colt, but he wasn't paying attention. "Where is she?" He'd lost sight of Natalie on the walk over.

"She's probably trotting Antwar around."

He met Jillian's gaze, realizing it was she who had spoken. "I thought she'd warmed up already."

"She's sixth to go, Colt. It'll be a bit of a wait."

Wait? What? He didn't want to wait. He wanted this to be over.

I love you, Colt.

He sank into the folding chair. Natalie loved him. He'd known she cared. He cared, too. It amazed him how much, given the short amount of time they'd known each other. Months. It didn't seem long enough.

The crowd inside the tent quieted. Colt realized a rider had entered the ring.

"Pretty horse," Mariah said.

Was it? He hardly noticed the big black gelding. He tried again to find Natalie, but she'd disappeared behind the row of horses, riders, grooms and spectators that lined the rail opposite where they sat. The starting horn sounded, causing Colt to jolt. The horse in the pen bolted, too.

"Looks like it might be a handful," Zach noted.

Colt's long-time friend turned out to be right and it was painful—agonizing, really—to watch the horse and rider gallop around. All Colt could think was what if Natalie had a similar ride? The horse she rode was young, and he knew it might act up, knew Natalie was out of practice. She'd ridden jumping horses for years, of course, but not recently.

He heard a thudding of hooves. One of the jumps had been set up right alongside the rail where they sat. A double set of poles, the holders made to look like wishing wells. A blue rubber mat had been placed underneath and Colt might not have known much about jumping, but he could tell the horse in the arena wanted nothing to do with it. The animal threw its head up, eyes wide with terror. The rider no doubt felt it too because Colt saw them go to the spur.

"Oh, that's not good."

Jillian's words turned out to be prophetic. The horse stopped. Hard. Colt gasped. The rider—a young woman, he realized, now that he could see her face— shot forward, but somehow, miraculously, managed to hang on.

"Too bad," Antwar's owner said. "She was having a nice go."

A nice go? Racing around the arena, barely in control, jumping willy-nilly over obstacles was a nice go?

He felt a hand on his arm. "Relax." Jillian smiled at him softly, reassuringly, green eyes full of faith. "These fences are nothing compared to what Natalie's used to jumping."

That was supposed to comfort him? He didn't care whether she took Antwar over something that was two feet tall or twenty. The point was these weren't sedate little quarter horses. These were hot-blooded, strong-necked young animals.

"My hands are shaking," he admitted.

Jillian's smile deepened the grooves near the corners of her eyes. "I get that way every time Wes competes."

"Wes doesn't jump."

"No. He just dives into herds of cows. Believe me, there are days when it feels every bit as dangerous."

Colt wasn't convinced, but he wasn't going to argue. Not when he feared opening his mouth might be all the invitation his lunch needed to make a hasty exit.

The next rider was no better. A big man riding a huge sorrel. He almost took out one of the pole holders that he overheard Mariah call a standard.

By the third horse Colt had a pretty good feel for the pattern. He put together all on his own that the jumps were marked in a way that made understanding the course pretty easy. Red flag on the right, white flag on the left. When the horse landed he could scan ahead and easily spot what should be the next obstacle. The pace seemed to be somewhere between a fast run and a gallop, although some horses seemed to move more slowly than others. Each rider was timed, he knew. If they went too slow they would be assessed a penalty. The goal was to make it around as quickly as possible with minimal penalties.

The fifth horse made it look easy, gliding effortlessly over the jumps, but Colt only watched part of his go. He noted another big sorrel in the distance, this one with white socks, a white blaze and a rider the size of a child on his back. There was applause when they finished, the first Colt had noticed, although Antwar's owner groaned.

"Time penalties," the older woman said. "Too slow. But only a one-point penalty. She's the leader so far."

Natalie appeared by the in gate.

She didn't glance in their direction. She was smiling at the woman on the sorrel. The two of them looked like something from a bygone era in their black habits, riding boots and breeches. They touched hands in a good-natured show of support as they passed each other.

Please, God, let her be safe.

Colt realized then that it'd been a long time since he'd prayed. Not even when Adam had been sick had he prayed. If he were honest with himself he had to admit to giving up on the man upstairs. His childhood had taught him that nothing could keep the devil from beating the crap out of you, not even God.

But he prayed then, with every fiber of his being. Prayed that Natalie's horse would behave. That nothing would go wrong.

She headed for the middle of the arena. Stopped.

"What's wrong?" he asked.

"Nothing," Jillian reassured him.

His friend was right. Natalie just stood there, letting her horse look around. She patted him as he scanned the arena and the jumps inside, his head lifted and his ears pricked forward.

"Smart." Antwar's owner seemed pleased. "Thank goodness she's competing again. Nobody has a feel for young horses like Natalie does."

She really did. Colt spotted how gently she touched the horse. How relaxed she seemed, which, in turn, caused the horse to calm down. How had he not noticed this about her before?

Because when she came to you she'd been terrified. Lost. Uncertain of her God-given abilities.

Out of the blue he felt his eyes begin to burn. They'd gotten her sorted out. No matter what the future held, he would always be pleased that he'd been able to help her overcome her fear of riding.

The horse in the arena lowered its head. Only then did Natalie gently squeeze it forward. The buzzer sounded and Colt knew she'd been given the go-ahead to start her course. Antwar knew it, too, lifting his head again, equine eyes scanning the jumps as Natalie cued the animal into a canter.

First jump. Red and white poles. Simple. Easy.

Natalie pointed Antwar in the jump's direction. She seemed to be standing in the stirrups, her upper body tilted forward, half-seat they called it. Colt reminded himself of her words.

I can keep my upper body from bouncing. It makes the dizziness go away.

Closer and closer they drew. He almost covered his eyes.

Antwar jumped perfectly.

"Lovely," said his owner.

Her pace wasn't as fast as the other riders, but it didn't need to be. The horse had a huge stride, Colt noticed, so big he made the jumps appear smaller. The next set, a long gallop down the middle of the ring, were a little taller. Antwar took them both effortlessly.

Around Natalie went, toward the opposite side of the rail. The flower jump, Colt had named it. Antwar lifted his head. Colt held his breath. At the last second the horse stumbled a bit.

Mariah gasped. Natalie tipped to one side. Antwar's knees came up to his eyeballs. One second, two, they hung in the air, Natalie somehow still in the saddle, until they disappeared on the other side.

Someone released a breath. Had it been him? Jillian? Colt didn't know. He didn't have time to breathe because the next set of jumps were right around the corner, another double set, this one close together. Antwar's big stride proved to be a problem. He saw Natalie check the animal before the jump. Once. Twice. They shot toward the wooden poles. When she landed she had to check him up again. One giant leap and they were off once more. Up and over the next jump. Cleanly. Safely. Brilliantly.

It was beautiful.

A calm settled over him. He watched her fly. An angel without wings. A Greek goddess riding Pegasus. Perfect.

Around the final turn they ran. Faster now. Natalie must have glanced at the clock, realized she was running out of time. Colt leaned forward in his seat, his heart pounding in rhythm to her horse's stride. The last jump was called a vertical. One row of poles. Deceptively easy, Jillian had told him earlier, meant to be the downfall of a good rider.

Natalie wasn't good. She was great.

Her hands were steady, the pressure of her legs tight. Five strides away. Four. Three. And then…

They jumped. Time stood still. Front legs first. Back legs next.

Perfect.

The crowd cheered. Natalie stood in her stirrups and lifted a fist in the air.

"She did it," Mariah said.

He glanced at the clock. No time penalties. She had, indeed, done it.

"Too early to know if she's won," Wes said.

"No," Colt heard himself say. He could feel everyone turn to look at him. "She's won."

He stood up, eyes only on Natalie. She pulled her horse into a walk, but he couldn't see her face. He wanted to see her face. Wanted to tell her that he understood now. Before today he'd had no idea what she'd given up. He'd known she was a good rider. He'd known there'd been talk about the games. She wasn't just good, though, she was great. Better even than he was.

And she'd been willing to give it up.

Because he'd told her to.

He pushed through the crowd. He heard someone yelp in disapproval. He could see Natalie nearing the out gate. He began to run. She must have said something to the next rider because they laughed as their horses passed each other. Natalie left the arena, walked forward a few steps and collapsed.

Colt yelled. Someone turned. Natalie wilted toward the ground.

No.

Someone caught her, though who it was Colt would never know. Hands grabbed the reins before Antwar could take off. A crowd formed around the fallen rider.

"Natalie."

He thought she'd passed out. Thought she might have had a stroke. Had the jumping jarred her brain injury? He slid through the ring of people.

She hadn't passed out. She sat on the ground, head in her hands.

And cried.

He nudged aside the stranger who'd caught her, muttered a quick thank you, and put his arms around Natalie. She went into them willingly. He pulled her into his lap. Held her. Squeezed her. Let her cry.

"Shh," he soothed. "It's okay."

When he caught a glimpse of the crowd, he saw she wasn't the only one who cried. Others stared down at her, tears on their lashes, too. It hit him then that these people knew. They'd known about her injury, that she'd been told not to ride. Known that she'd given it up, at least temporarily. Just as they knew the tears she shed were ones of joy, not sorrow.

She'd overcome. Conquered her fear. Done the impossible and learned to ride all over again.

He drew back. She did, too.

"You are such an idiot," he admonished.

Beneath her riding hat he saw her eyes widen.

"Thanks," she sniffed, wiping at her tears. "I love you, too."

Yes. She did love him, and he loved her. More than life itself. As much as he loved his nephew and his sister and his brother all combined. A different kind of love. A love he'd known was there, but never admitted—just as his sister had said.

Natalie must have seen it in his eyes because her smile lit up her face like the summer sun turning the heavens a million shades of gold. He kissed her again and she *did* know. He might have a hard time saying the words, but she knew what he was trying to tell her. It was the only way he knew how to say what was deep in his heart. With his mouth and his hands and his touch. Silently. Without words.

"Finally," he heard someone say.

He looked up. Sam stared at him with tears in her eyes. So did Mariah and Zach and Jillian and Wes. And Randy, too.

"'Bout time," Wes said.

Yes. It was about time.

He finally understood what it meant to overcome fear. Understood what it meant to love. Understood how lucky he was.

"Marry me," he heard himself say.

Natalie stiffened in his arms. For a moment he worried she might say no. That she didn't love him that much.

Her eyes softened. "Only if you promise never to make me ride Western again."

He laughed. He couldn't help himself. She started to laugh, too. So did Wes and the gang around them. And then there were pats and cheers and good-natured slaps on the back. They stood. Together. Side by side.

The way they would stand for the rest of their lives.

Epilogue

Helicopters circled overhead.

Natalie looked out Colt's kitchen window and wondered for the hundredth time why the paparazzi felt the need to intrude on Adam's special day.

"Better hurry up. People are starting to arrive." It was Claire who'd spoken, looking as bright and beautiful as a daffodil in her sleeveless yellow dress. "I just had a chat with last year's best actress."

It had been Adam's idea. The little boy had improved to the point that they'd released him from the hospital. He wasn't out of the woods quite yet—cancer couldn't be cured overnight—but his treatment plan had been deemed a success so far. And they were lucky. Nothing had metastasized. All good news. So, when one of his sick friends had mentioned his mom couldn't sit with him for treatment because she couldn't afford to hire a babysitter, Adam had been horrified. Claire had explained how they had a network of friends and family to help out, but not everyone did. That had lit a new fire in Adam's heart.

Coins for Caring had been born.

"The caterers just warmed up some more of those bacon onion ball thingies." Natalie tried to wipe the guilty look off her face. "Oh, my goodness, they are to die for." She reached for the tray, preparing to bring it outside, but Claire stayed her with a hand.

"Before you leave, I wanted to say something."

Natalie straightened in surprise.

"I know all this—" she waved a hand around her "—couldn't be easy."

"What do you mean? I'm happy to help out."

Claire shook her head. "No." She took a deep breath. "I mean coming into a family that has more baggage than an airport on Christmas Day." She smiled ruefully. "Dealing with Colt and his issues. Then having to deal with Colt's sick nephew." She had pulled her long, black hair away from her face, exposing green eyes that had gone dark with serious-ness. "Now this." She swung a hand toward Colt's front yard.

"This" was every A-list celebrity Randy knew. Coins for Caring had morphed from a donation jar at Children's Hospital to an all-day event held at Reyn-olds's Ranch. Claire was right. It'd been a little crazy.

"Are you kidding? All this is great."

A concert would be held later on, performed by some little teeny-bopper band Natalie had never heard of, but that was clearly incredibly popular because tickets for the day's event had sold out in less than an hour. There would be a performance by Colt and the Galloping Girlz in the afternoon, a silent auction, and the coup de grâce, a live auction where none other than Rand Jefferson would be auctioned off for a day.

"Still. This can't be easy."

Natalie waved her hand, the engagement ring Colt had bought her shortly after she'd won the Gucci Mini

Prix sparkling. "Colt and I wouldn't have it any other way."

"So you say." Claire's eyes held her own. The gratitude mixed with love made a lump form in Natalie's throat. "But I appreciate it all the same."

Natalie leaned forward and impulsively pulled Claire into her arms. She'd never had the love and support of a sibling, but she did now.

"Hey." They pulled apart as Colt entered the kitchen with a smile. "What's going on in here? Way too much to do for you two to be loitering around."

"Loitering," Claire teased. "Hardly."

Natalie and Colt watched as she walked out. "It's good to see her with a smile on her face," Colt observed.

Yes, it was. The poor woman had been through far too much in life. This latest blow might have driven a lot of people over the edge. Not Claire. She continued to drive her son back and forth to doctor's appointments, volunteer countless hours on behalf of Combat Pet Rescue and still maintain her spirits.

"She's incredible," Natalie reflected.

"Almost as incredible as you." Colt reached for her, one hand entwining with her own, the other cupping her cheek. "Last night was unbelievable."

She wasn't prone to blushing, but the way he looked into her eyes made her skin catch fire. "Yeah, well, wait until our wedding night."

She knew her voice had gone husky with pent up desire, but damn it, this abstinence thing was torture. They'd been holding off, waiting until they were husband and wife, something they hadn't planned, but had seemed right somehow. But that didn't mean they couldn't act like teenagers now and then.

"I'm looking forward to—"

"Colt," Wes interrupted, popping his head in the kitchen through the side door, sunshine silhouetting his shape into a shadow, cowboy hat and all. "One of the band members is looking for a 240 outlet. Do you have one they can plug into?"

And right behind Wes, Mariah. "Natalie, I need duct tape. The plastic table tops are blowing around."

Natalie and Colt exchanged amused glances. It was like a shot from a starting gun. For the next few hours they ran. Directing traffic, greeting guests and, most importantly, helping to raise money. When it came time for Colt to perform, Natalie felt lucky to squeeze in a moment to watch.

"I told you he was amazing," Jillian said, coming up next to her—quite a feat given Colt's arena seemed to have more people packed around it than a high school football game.

"You were right," Natalie murmured.

"Of course, you're pretty amazing yourself."

Colt was just getting to the part where he would drag out the ring for Sam to jump through. Sam, the woman who'd managed to capture the heart of Hollywood's newest "it" man—much to the chagrin of women the world over.

"What is this? Ply Natalie with compliments day?"

"What do you mean?"

But Natalie made sure Jillian knew she wasn't serious. "Earlier Claire and I were talking about what a saint I am, but I'm not complaining." She glanced back at the arena, watching as Colt removed the soon-to-be flaming hoop from the trailer. "Go on. Sing my praises."

From the rail, she heard Jillian chuckle. "Well when you put it that way, forget it."

Natalie would have let the matter drop, but Jillian said, "Seriously. You're an inspiration. Not only did you compete in your first reining competition this past month, but you're back on track to qualify for international competition."

"No," Natalie said. "I wouldn't go quite that far yet. There's still some work to do."

But it wasn't the dizzy spells she had to worry about. Those had disappeared the day she'd ridden in the mini prix. Psychosomatic, her neurologists had concluded, which explained why they had never been able to find a physical cause for them. She'd been given the all clear to ride again, and despite her quip to Colt, she'd continued her training with Playboy, relishing her success at a reining competition. Her neurologist had cautioned that show jumping was a dangerous sport, though. She knew that, but Colt supported her 100 percent. Once they were married they planned to build a state-of-the-art training facility at the ranch. A place to call her own. A place that she and Colt could maintain and love—no matter if she had fifty clients or five.

"Who would have known that day you introduced Colt to me it would change my life."

Jillian glanced at her friend. "No," she said softly. "You changed his."

Natalie slipped an arm around her friend's shoulders and whispered in her ear, "If I tell you a secret will you promise not to tell?"

Jillian drew back sharply. "You're pregnant."

Natalie laughed. "Not possible." She shook her head, lowered her voice again. Around her, the crowd seemed oblivious, their gazes fixed on the performers in the middle of the arena. Colt had just lit the hoop on fire, Sam peeling off for the finale of the show.

"Not pregnant." She smiled. "Getting married." And her heart suddenly filled with love. "Tonight."

"Tonight!"

"Shh." Natalie glanced around, not that anyone noticed. "After everyone's gone. Well, after last year's Grammy winners leave, and their celebrity friends and what seems like half of Santa Barbara County."

"You're kidding."

"This time tomorrow morning, we'll be Mr. and Mrs. Colton Reynolds."

In the arena Sam headed toward the hoop, and just as it always did, Natalie's breath caught. Or maybe she couldn't breathe because she knew that in less than twenty-four hours, the man inside the arena would be hers at last.

Jillian squeezed her. Hard. "I'm so glad."

"We figured, why not. Everyone's already here. The caterer gave us a deal and the place is all decorated."

"It'll be perfect."

And it was. Natalie didn't know who told the band—probably Jillian—but once they heard there would be a wedding, nothing could persuade them to leave. And so, beneath a starry sky, with friends and family and more than a few celebrities watching, Natalie married Colt in a ceremony that couldn't have been more perfect if they'd tried.

"I just wish Chance could have been here," Colt whispered as they danced.

"He's here in spirit."

Colt's brother was currently deployed, but he'd told Colt last night that he wouldn't be reenlisting. By the end of the year he'd be back at the ranch. Colt couldn't wait to welcome his brother back into the fold.

"Can I have this dance?" Wes asked after tapping Colt on the shoulder.

"No," Colt said, sounding like his surly old self as he whisked Natalie away.

She laughed. "That wasn't nice."

He leaned down close to her, his cowboy hat brushing the top of her veil. "I can't help it," he whispered in her ear. "I'm not a very nice person."

She rested her head on his shoulder. "I hope not, Mr. Reynolds. In fact, I'm counting on you being very naughty tonight."

"Oh, I will be," he reassured her, but she could hear the laughter in his voice. "I plan to do all kinds of wicked things to you later this evening."

And later that night he did exactly as promised, the two of them sharing a night made all the more special by how long they'd waited. It was the first of many such nights, nights they would never again spend alone.

* * * * *

A HOME FOR CHRISTMAS

Laura Marie Altom

"Rachel!"

Ignoring Chance Mulgrave, her husband's best friend, Rachel Finch gripped her umbrella handle as if it were the only thing keeping her from throwing herself over the edge of the cliff, at the base of which thundered an angry Pacific. Even for Oregon Coast standards, the day was hellish. Brutal winds, driving cold rain...

The wailing gloom suited her. Only ten minutes earlier, she'd left the small chapel where her presumed dead husband's memorial service had just been held.

"Please, Rachel!" Chance shouted above the storm. Rachel didn't see Chance since her back was to him, but she could feel him thumping toward her on crutches. "Honey..."

He cupped his hand to her shoulder and she flinched, pulling herself free of his hold. "Don't."

"Sure," he said. "Whatever. I just—"

She turned to him, too exhausted to cry. "I'm pregnant."

"What?"

"Wes didn't know. I'd planned on telling him after he'd finished this case."

"God, Rache." Sharing the suffocating space beneath her umbrella, his demeanor softened. "I'm sorry. Or maybe happy. Hell, I'm not sure what to say."

"There's not much anyone can say at this point," she responded. "Wes is gone. I'm having his child… but how can I even think of being a mother when I'm so emotionally…"

"Don't worry about a thing," he said. "No matter what you need, I'm here for you. Wes and I made a pact. Should anything happen to either of us, we'd watch after each other's family."

"But you don't have a family," she pointed out.

"Yet. But it could've just as easily been me whose life we were celebrating here today." He bowed his head. "Seeing you like this…so sad…makes me almost wish it was."

Me, too.

There. Even if Rachel hadn't given voice to her resentment, it was at least out there, for the universe to hear. Ordinarily, Chance and her husband worked together like a well-oiled team, watching each other's backs. But then Chance had had to go and bust his ankle while helping one of their fellow deputy US marshals move into a new apartment.

If Chance had really cared for Wes, he'd have been more careful. He wouldn't have allowed his friend to be murdered at the hands of a madman—a rogue marshal who'd also come uncomfortably close to taking out one of the most key witnesses the Marshal's Service had ever had.

Her handful of girlfriends had tried consoling her, suggesting maybe Wes wasn't really dead…but Rachel knew. There had been an exhaustive six-week search for Wes's body. Combined with that, of the five marshals who'd been on that assignment, only two had come home alive. Another two bodies had been found, both shot. It didn't take rocket science to assume the same had happened to her dear husband.

"Let me take you home," Chance said. Despite his crutches, he tried to angle her away from the thrashing sea and back to the parking lot, to the sweet little chapel where less than a year earlier she and Wes had spoken their wedding vows.

"You're soaked. Being out here in this weather can't be good for you or the baby."

"I'm all right," she said, again wrenching free of his hold. This time, it had been her elbow he'd grasped. She was trying to regain her dignity after having lost it in front of the church filled with Wes's coworkers and friends, and she just wanted to be left alone. "Please…leave. I can handle this on my own."

"Rachel, that's just it," he said, awkwardly chasing after her as she strode down the perilous trail edging the cliff.

His every step tore at her heart. Why was he alive and not her husband? The father of her child. What was she going to do? How was she ever going to cope with raising a baby on her own?

"Honey, you don't have to deal with Wes's passing on your own. If you'd just open up to me, I'm here for you—for as long as you need."

That was the breaking point. Rachel stopped abruptly. She tossed her umbrella out to sea, tipped her head up to the battering rain and screamed.

Tears returned with a hot, messy vengeance. Only,

in the rain it was impossible to tell where tears left off and rain began. Then, suddenly, Chance was there, drawing her against him, into his island of strength and warmth, his crutches braced on either side of her like walls blocking the worst of her pain.

"That's it," he crooned into her ear. "Let it out. I'm here. I'm here."

She did exactly as he urged, but then, because she'd always been an intensely private person and not one prone to histrionics, she stilled. Curiously, the rain and wind also slowed to a gentle patter and hushed din.

"Thank you," she eventually said. "You'll never know how much I appreciate you trying to help, but…"

"I'm not just trying," he said. "If you'd let me in, we can ride this out together. I'm hurting, too."

"I know," she said, looking to where she'd white-knuckle gripped the soaked lapels of his buff-colored trench. "But I—I can't explain. I have to do this on my own. I was alone before meeting Wes, and now I am again."

"But you don't have to be. Haven't you heard a word I've said? I'm here for you."

"No," she said, walking away from him again, this time in the direction of her car.

"Thanks, but definitely, no."

Eighteen months later…

THROUGH THE RAIN-DRIZZLED, holiday-themed windows of bustling Hohlmann's Department Store, Chance caught sight of a woman's long, buttery-blond hair.

Heart pounding, his first instinct was to run toward her, seeking an answer to the perpetual question: Was it her? Was it Rachel?

No. It wasn't her. And this time, just as so many others, the disappointment landed like a crushing blow to his chest.

That day at the chapel had been the last time he'd seen her. Despite exhaustive efforts to track her, she'd vanished—destroying him inside and out.

When eventually he'd had to return to work and his so-called normal life, he'd put a private investigator on retainer, telling the man to contact him upon finding the slightest lead.

"You all right?" his little sister, nineteen-year-old Sarah, asked above an obnoxious Muzak rendition of "Jingle Bells." She was clutching the prewrapped perfume box she'd just purchased for their mother. "You look like you've seen a ghost."

"Might as well have," he said, taking the box from her to add to his already bulging bag. "Got everything you need?"

"Sure," she said, giving him the *Look*. The one that said she knew he was thinking about Rachel again, and that her wish for Christmas was that her usually wise big brother would once and for all put the woman—his dead best friend's wife—out of his heart and head.

Two hours later, Chance stuck his key in the lock of the Victorian relic his maternal grandmother had left him, shutting out hectic holiday traffic and torrential rain. Portland had been swamped under six inches in the past twenty-four hours. The last time they'd had such a deluge had been the last time he'd seen Rachel.

"Where are you?" he asked softly as the wind bent gnarled branches, eerily scratching them against the back porch roof.

Setting his meager selection of family gifts on the wood bench parked alongside the door, he looked away from the gray afternoon and to the blinking light on his answering machine. Expecting the message to be from Sarah, telling him she'd left a gift or glove in his Jeep, he pressed Play.

"Chance," his PI said, voice like gravel from too many cigarettes and not enough broccoli. "I've got a lead for you on that missing Finch girl. It's a long shot, but you said you wanted everything, no matter how unlikely…"

Despite the fact that Rachel had run off without the decency of a proper—or even improper—goodbye, her tears still haunted him when he closed his eyes.

Chance listened to the message three times before committing the information to memory, then headed to his computer to book a flight to Denver.

"WESLEY, SWEETIE, PLEASE stop crying," Rachel crooned to her ten-month-old baby boy, the only bright spot in what was becoming an increasingly frightening life. Having grown up in an orphanage, Rachel was no stranger to feeling alone in a crowd, or having to make it on her own. So why, after six months, was this still so hard?

Despite her hugging and cooing, the boy only wailed more.

"Want me to take him?"

She looked up to see one of Baker Street Homeless Shelter's newest residents wave grungy hands toward her child. She hadn't looked much better when she'd first arrived, and Rachel still couldn't get past the shock that she and her baby were now what most people would call *bums*.

After reverting back to the name she'd gone by at the orphanage, Rachel Parkson, she'd traveled to Denver to room with her friend Jenny. But while Jenny had gotten lucky, landing a great job transfer to Des Moines, Rachel had descended into an abyss of bad luck.

A tough pregnancy had landed her in hospital. While she'd been blessed with a beautiful, healthy baby, at the rate she was going, the hefty medical bill wouldn't be gone till he was out of high school. Wes's life insurance company had repeatedly denied her claim, stating that without a body it wouldn't pay.

Making a long, sad story short, she'd lost everything, and here she was, now earning less than minimum wage doing bookkeeping for the shelter while trying to finish her business degree one night course at a time through a downtown Denver community college.

She was raising her precious son in a shelter with barely enough money for diapers, let alone food and a place of their own. She used to cry herself to sleep every night, but now, she was just too exhausted. She used to pray, as well, but it seemed God, just like her husband, had deserted her.

Baby Wesley continued to wail.

"Sorry for all the noise," she said to the poor soul beside her, holding her son close as she wearily pushed to her feet with her free hand. She had to get out of here, but how? How could she ever escape this downward financial spiral?

"Rachel?"

That voice…

She paused before looking up. But when she did, tingles climbed her spine.

"Chance?"

AFTER ALL THIS TIME, was it really Rachel? Raising Wes's child in a homeless shelter? Why, why hadn't she just asked for help?

Chance pressed the heel of his hand to stinging eyes.

"Y-you look good," he said, lying through his teeth at the waiflike ghost of the woman he used to know. Dark shadows hollowed pale blue eyes. Wes used to brag about the silky feel of Rachel's long hair cascading against his chest when they'd made love—but it was now shorn into a short cap. "And the baby. He's wonderful, Rachel. You did good."

"Thanks," she said above her son's pitiful cry. "We're okay." She paused. "What are you doing here?"

"I'm here to see you… To help you…"

"I don't need help."

"Bull," he said, taking the now screaming baby from her, cradling him against his chest, nuzzling the infant's downy hair beneath his chin. "What's his name?"

"Wesley," she said, refusing to meet his gaze.

He nodded, fighting a sudden knot at the back of his throat. Such a beautiful child, growing up in such cruel surroundings. And why? All because of Rachel's foolish pride.

"Get your things," he growled between clenched teeth, edging her away from a rag-clothed derelict reeking of booze.

"W-what?"

"You heard me. You tried things your way, honey, and apparently it didn't work out. Now we're doing it *my* way. Your husband's way."

"I— I'm fine," she said, raising her chin, a partial spark back in her stunning eyes. "Just a little down on my luck. But things will change. They'll get better."

"Damn straight they will." Clutching the infant with one arm, he dragged her toward the shelter's door with the other. "You don't want charity from me, fine. But is this really what you want for your son? Wes's son?"

While Chance regretted the harshness of his words, he'd never retract them. Years ago he'd made a promise to her husband, and he sure as hell wasn't about to back out on it now.

He glanced away from Rachel to take in a nearly bald, fake Christmas tree that'd been decorated with homemade ornaments. Pipe cleaner reindeer and paper angels colored with crayons. Though the tree's intent was kind, he knew Rachel deserved better.

While killing time on endless stakeouts, Wes would ramble for hours about his perfect wife. About how much he loved her, how she was a great cook, how she always managed to perfectly balance the checkbook. Wes went so far as to offer private morsels he should've kept to himself—locker room details that should've been holy between a man and his wife.

But because of Wes's ever-flapping mouth, whether he'd wanted to or not, Chance knew everything about Rachel from her favorite songs to what turned her on.

Another thing he knew were Wes's dreams for her. How because she'd grown up in an orphanage, he'd always wanted to have a half-dozen chubby babies with her and buy her a great house and put good, reliable tires on her crappy car.

Chance had made a promise to his best friend; one that put him in charge of picking up where Wes left off. It was a given he'd steer clear of the husband-wife physical intimacies—she was off-limits. Totally. But when it came to making her comfortable, happy…by God, if it took every day for the rest of his life, that's what Chance had come to Denver prepared—and okay, he'd admit it, secretly hoping—to do.

Looking back to Rachel, he found her eyes pooled. Lips trembling, she met his stare.

"Come on," he said. "It's time to go home."

Baby Wesley had fallen asleep in Chance's arms. His cheeks were flushed, and he sucked pitifully at his thumb.

"I—I tried breastfeeding him," she said. "But my milk dried up."

"That happens," he said, not knowing if it did or didn't or why she'd even brought it up…just willing to say anything to get her to go with him.

Shaking her head, looking away to brush tears, she said, "Wait here. I'll get our things."

For Rachel, being at the airport and boarding the plane was surreal. As was driving through a fog-shrouded Portland in Chance's Jeep, stopping off at an all-night Walmart for a car seat and over five hundred dollars' worth of clothes, diapers, formula and other baby supplies. The Christmas decorations, hundreds and thousands of colorful lights lining each new street they traveled, struck her as foreign. As if from a world where she was no longer welcome.

"I'll repay you," she said from the passenger seat, swirling a pattern in the fogged window. Presumably, he was heading toward his lovely hilltop home she'd always secretly called the real estate version of a wedding cake. "For everything. The clothes. Plane ticket. I'll pay it all back. I—I just need a breather to get back on my feet."

"Sure," he said. Was it her imagination, or had he tightened his grip on the wheel?

"Really," she said, rambling on about how Wes's life insurance company refused to pay. "Just as soon as I get the check, I'll reimburse you."

"Know how you can pay me?" he asked, pressing the garage door remote on the underbelly of his sun visor.

She shook her head.

He pulled the Jeep into the single-stall detached garage she'd helped Wes and him build, that same enchanted summer she and her future husband had become lovers.

It is said a woman's heart is a deep well of secrets and Rachel knew hers was no different. Squeezing her eyes shut, she saw Chance as she had that first night they'd met at Ziggy's Sports Bar—before she'd even met Wes. Despite his physical appearance— six-three, with wide, muscular shoulders and a chest as broad and strong as an oak's trunk—Chance's shy, kind spirit made him a gentle giant to whom she'd instinctively gravitated.

Never the brazen type, Rachel had subtly asked mutual friends about him, and every so often, when their eyes met from opposite ends of the bar during the commercial breaks of *Monday Night Football*, she'd thought she'd caught a glimmer of interest. And if only for an instant, hope that he might find her as attractive as she found him would soar. But then he'd look away and the moment would be gone.

Then she'd met Wes—who'd made it known in about ten exhilaratingly sexy seconds that he didn't just want to be her *friend*. Handsome, five-eleven with a lean build and quick smile, Wes hadn't had to work too hard to make her fall for him—or to make any and all occasions magic.

Chance turned off the engine and sighed. The only light was that which spilled from the weak bulb attached to the automatic opener, the only sounds those of rain pattering the roof and the baby's sleepy gurgle... Angling on his seat, Chance reached out to Rachel, whispering the tip of his index finger so softly around her lips...she might've imagined his being there at all.

"Know how you can repay me?" he repeated.

Heartbeat a sudden storm, she swallowed hard.

"By bringing back your smile."

RACHEL AWOKE THE next morning to unfamiliar softness, and the breezy scent of freshly laundered sheets. Sunshine streamed through tall paned windows. After a moment of initial panic, fearing she may have died and moved on to heaven, she remembered herself not on some random cloud, but safely tucked in Chance's guest bed in the turret-shaped room she'd urged him to paint an ethereal sky blue.

The room was the highest point in his home, reached by winding stairs, and its view never failed to stir her. Mt. Hood was to the west, while to the east— long ago, while standing on a ladder, paint brush in hand, nose and cheeks smudged blue—she'd sworn she could see all the way to the shimmering Pacific. Wesley and Chance had laughed at her, but she'd ignored them.

To Rachel, the room represented freedom from all that had bound her in her early, depressing, pre-Wes life. The panoramic views, just as her marriage, made her feel as if her soul was flying.

As she inched up in the sumptuous feather bed to greet a day as chilly as it was clear, the room still wielded its calming effect. She'd awakened enough to realize how late it must be…and yet Wesley hadn't stirred.

Tossing back covers, she winced at the wood floor's chilly bite against her bare feet. With one look at the portable crib that had been among their purchases the previous night, Rachel realized that Wesley's cries hadn't woken her because he wasn't there.

Bounding to the kitchen, she found her son sitting proud in his new high chair, beaming, covered ear to ear in peachy-smelling orange goo.

"Morning, sleepyhead." Baby spoon to Wesley's cooing lips, Chance caught her off guard with the size of his smile.

"You should've woken me," she said, hustling to where the two guys sat at a round oak table in a sunny patch of the country kitchen. "I'm sure you have better things to do."

"Nope," he said. "I took the day off."

"I'll pay you for your time."

He'd allowed her to take the spoon as she'd pulled out a chair and sat beside him, but now, his strong fingers clamped her wrist. "Stop."

"What?"

"The whole defensive routine. It doesn't become you."

"S-sorry. That's who I am."

"Bull."

"E-excuse me?" He released her, and the spoon now trembled in her still tingling wrist.

"I knew you as playful. Fun. Now, you seem like you're in attack mode."

"And why shouldn't I be?" she asked. "Aside from Wesley, name one thing that's gone right for me in the past year?"

"That's easy," he said, cracking a slow and easy grin that, Lord help her, had Rachel's pulse racing yet again. Had the man always been this attractive?

Judging by the massive crush she'd had on him all those years ago…yes.

Making things worse—or better, depending how you looked at it—he winked. "One thing that's gone very right is how you're finally back with me."

Sensing Rachel needed two gifts above all else that Christmas season—time and space—Chance returned to work Tuesday, and every day for the rest of the week. Come Saturday, though, despite her protests that they should stay at the house, he bustled her and the baby into his Jeep and started off for the traditional holiday ride he'd loved as a kid, but had given up as an adult.

"Well?" he asked a silent Rachel an hour later, pulling into a snow-covered winter wonderland. "See anything that'd fit in the living room bay window?"

She glanced at him, then at the sprawling Christmas tree farm that might as well have been Santa's North Pole as everywhere you looked, Christmas was in full swing. Kids laughing and sledding and playing tag while darting in and out amongst fragrant trees. Families hugging the fires built in river rock pits, sipping steaming mugs of cocoa. Upbeat carols played from a tiny speaker.

"It's—" she cautiously glanced at the idyllic scene before them, as if they didn't belong, then back to him "—amazing. But if you want a tree, wouldn't it be cheaper to—"

"Look—" he sighed "—I wasn't going to bring this up until it's a done deal, but I told my boss about your situation—with Wes's flaky life insurance—and fury didn't begin to describe his reaction. Wheels are turning, and I'd say you'll have a check by the end of next week."

"Really?"

Just then, she was seriously gorgeous, eyes brimming with hope and a shimmering lake of tears. "Yeah," Chance said. "I'm serious. So what's with the waterworks? I thought you'd be thrilled to be rich?"

"I would be—I mean, I am. It's just that after all these months of barely scraping by, not sleeping because I've literally been afraid to close my eyes, it seems a bit surreal to have such a happy ending at all, let alone in such a happy place."

He laughed, unfastening his seat belt to grab the baby from his seat. "Don't you think after what you've been through you two deserve a little happiness?"

She turned away from him while she sniffled and dried her cheeks, and he couldn't tell if she was nodding or shaking her head. "Well?" he asked. "Was that a yes or no?"

"I don't know," she said with a laugh. "Maybe both. I'm just so confused. And grateful. Very, *very* grateful."

"Yeah, well, what you need to be," he said, Wesley snug in his arms, "is energized."

"Oh, yeah?" she asked, again blasting him with a tremulous smile. "How come?"

"Because me and this kid of yours are about to *whomp* you in a snowball fight."

"IT's BEAUTIFUL," RACHEL SAID, stepping back to admire the nine-foot fir they'd finished decorating. Heirloom glass ornaments and twinkling white lights hung from each branch. "Perfect."

With Chance beside her, carols softly playing and a fire crackling in the hearth, Rachel couldn't have ordered a more enchanting holiday scene.

"I don't know," Chance said, finger to his lips as he stood beside her, surveying their afternoon's work. "Something's missing."

"You're right," Rachel said. "We forgot the angel."

"I didn't see it, did you?"

"Not in the boxes we've been through. Maybe—"

She looked down to see Wesley sucking the top corner of the angel's box. "Aha! Found it."

"Thanks, bud." Chance took the box from the baby, replacing it with the teething ring he had been contentedly gumming. "How about you do the honors?" he suggested, handing the golden angel to her.

"I'd like that," Rachel said, embarrassed to admit just how much the small gesture meant.

At the orphanage, placing the angel on top of the tree was generally a task reserved for the child who was newest to the home. Since Rachel had gone to live there the summer just before her fourth birthday when her parents had been killed in a car accident, she'd never had the chance. By the time Christmas rolled around, she had only been the third-newest kid.

Knowing this, Wes had made their first Christmas together as a married couple extra special by taking her to pick out an especially extravagant angel that they really couldn't afford. In Denver, at a desperation yard sale she'd held in a futile attempt to stay financially afloat, it had devastated her to have to sell that precious angel to a cranky old guy for the princely sum of three dollars.

Rachel swallowed hard at the bittersweet memory of how dearly she'd loved sharing Christmas with Wes. There was a part of her struggling with the guilt that she was once again immersed in holiday cheer… but Wes was gone. It somehow felt disloyal for her to be so happy.

Trying to focus on the task at hand, Rachel climbed onto the small stepladder she'd used to hang the ornaments from the highest branches, but she still wasn't tall enough to reach the tree's top.

"Let me help," Chance said, inching up behind her, settling his hands around her waist, then lifting her the extra inches needed to get the job done.

His nearness was overwhelming, flooding her senses to the point she nearly failed her mission. Had his hands lingered on her waist longer than necessary after he'd set her back to her feet? Was that the reason for her erratically beating heart? What kind of woman was she to one minute reminisce about her deceased husband, and the next wonder at the feel of another man's strong hands?

"Thank you," she said, licking her lips, going by habit to push back her long hair that was no longer there.

"You're welcome." As if he'd sensed the awareness between them, too, they both fell into awkward step, bustling to clean the wreckage of tissue paper and boxes.

Once they'd finished hauling the mess to a spare bedroom Chance used for storage, they were in the dark upstairs hall when Chance asked, "Why'd you cut your hair?"

The question caught her off guard, made her feel even more uncomfortable than she already did. "It was too much trouble," she said.

"It was beautiful. Not that it's any of my business, but you should grow it back."

She looked down to hands she'd clenched at her waist.

"Not that you aren't still attractive," he said. "It's just that Wes always had a thing for your hair. I think he'd be sad to see it gone."

What about you, Chance? Did you like my hair?

Rachel was thankful for the hall's lack of light—the question, even if asked only in her head, made her uncomfortable. Why would she even care what Chance thought of the way she used to style her hair? Worse yet, why did his question leave her feeling lacking?

Suddenly, she was wishing she at least had a little more length to work into an attractive style instead of the boyish cut that'd been easy to keep clean and neat at the homeless shelter. This cut hardly made her feel feminine or desirable. But then until her reunion with Chance, she'd had no use for vanity.

"Chance?" she asked, her voice a croaked whisper.

"Yes?"

"When we first met, you know, back when you, me and Wes used to just be friends, hanging out at Ziggy's, did you find me pretty?"

He cleared his throat. "What kind of question is that?"

"I don't know." She shook her head. "Sorry I asked."

Because she truly didn't know, Rachel returned to the living room, where holiday cheer and the sight of her contented child banished doubts and fears. The question had been silly. As was her growing awareness of her late husband's best friend. For a moment she felt better, but then Chance returned, his essence filling the room.

"For the record," he said, perching alongside her on the toasty fireplace hearth, "yes. I thought you were pretty back then, but you're even prettier now."

CHANCE HAD A tough time finding sleep. Why had Rachel asked him such a loaded question? Why did he feel his final, almost flirty answer had been a betrayal of his friend's trust? Yeah, Chance thought she was pretty—gorgeous, in fact. But for Wes's sake, couldn't he have just skirted the issue?

Sunday morning, he woke to a breakfast spread fit for a five-star hotel. "Wow," he said. "What's all this for?"

Looking more gorgeous than any woman had a right to first thing in the morning, she shrugged. "Guess I just wanted to say thanks for the great day we had yesterday. Never having had a family growing up, I always wished for that kind of traditional family fun."

"Is that what we are?" he asked, forking a bite of pancake. "A family?"

"You know what I mean," she said, avoiding his glance by drinking orange juice.

He broke off a piece of bacon and handed it to Wesley.

"Yeah," he said. "I know what you mean. But *is* that what we are, Rache?"

Sitting with her and Wesley, from out of nowhere Chance was struck with the realization that no matter how she answered his question, he very much *wanted* them to be a family. They'd already fallen into husband and wife roles. The only things missing were emotional and physical closeness.

And as reluctant as he was to admit it, from the day he'd set eyes on her all those years ago, kissing Rachel was something he'd always longed to do. And therein lay the rub. Somehow, he had to find it within himself to squelch that want.

"We're sort of a family," she said. "But I suppose,

once I get Wes's life insurance you'll probably be glad to get the house back to yourself."

Boldly reaching across the table for her hand, stroking her palm, lying to himself by labeling it a casual, friendly touch, he said, "Actually, it's nice having you two here. Waking up to you in the morning, coming home to you at night."

She laughed off his admission. "You're just being polite. No bachelor actually enjoys being strapped with another man's wife and child."

"That's just it," he said. "Crazy as it may seem, I like you being here—a lot."

ANOTHER WEEK PASSED, during which Rachel had too much time to ponder Chance's curious statement. He liked having her and Wesley sharing his house? If only he truly felt that way because, truth be told, she liked being there, and judging by Wesley's easy grins, he did, too.

Being with Chance made her feel safe—an emotion that'd been sorely lacking from the past eighteen months of her life. Being with him now told her what a fool she'd been for ever denying his offer of help and companionship. He was a wonderful man.

The only reason she was now standing at the front window on a sunny Friday afternoon, watching for his Jeep to head up the winding lane leading to his home was because she was thankful to him…right? No way could it be something more.

Trouble was, try as she might to pass off the growing feelings she had for him as simply affection between friends, she *did* feel something more. Twinges of attraction. Flickering flames.

Whatever the label, it had wrongfully been there Sunday morning when he'd held her hand across the breakfast table. And Monday night when their hands brushed while Chance helped with Wesley's bath. Again still Tuesday and Wednesday when they'd shared the usually dull duty of cleaning up after dinner.

Instead of being ho-hum, washing dishes with Chance towering beside her, making her feel small and cherished and protected, had been—in a word—*intoxicating*.

But why? Why couldn't she keep at the forefront of her mind the fact that Chance had been Wes's best friend? To follow through on any attraction for him would be wrong.

Finally, she saw him pulling into the drive. Though she wanted to run to the back door to greet him like a giddy school girl, she somehow managed to rein in her emotions. Instead, with Wesley in her arms, she checked on the latest fragrant batch of sugar cookies still in the oven.

"Smells wonderful in here," Chance said with a gorgeous grin on his way through the back door. "You must be psychic."

"Why's that?" she asked, telling herself the heat from the oven had her cheeks flushed—not the pleasure of being the recipient of his smile.

"My parents invited us for dinner. Sugar cookies are Dad's favorite—not that he'll need a reason to fall for you or my buddy Wesley." After slipping off his coat, then setting his keys and wallet on the blue tile counter, he took the baby from her, swooping him high into the air, then snug against his chest for a cuddle and kiss. "Mmm… I missed you," he said, nuzzling the infant's head.

Rachel fought irrational jealousy strumming through her as she realized she wanted Chance to have missed her, too. Almost as much as she wanted a welcome home kiss…

RELAXING OVER ALMOND Bundt cake and coffee with Chance's mother, Helen, while the men washed up after dinner, Rachel would've had a hard time remembering a time she'd ever felt more content.

Helen had decorated her home from top to bottom in holiday decor ranging from elegant to goofy fun. The crackling fire and Elvis CD of holiday love songs playing softly in the background only made the night that much more special.

"Please don't think me forward for bringing this up," Helen said after they'd had a few moments to finish their cake, "but my son's a different person around you and Wesley. Better, in every conceivable way."

Rachel was so caught off guard by the woman's random statement that she darned near choked on her last bite of dessert. "Oh?"

"He loves you, you know. Has loved you ever since you first met all those years ago. Bless his heart…" She paused for a sip of coffee. "He was always the strong, silent type. His father and I urged him to tell you how he felt before you and Wes grew close, but he missed his window of opportunity and seeing how he and Wes were always such good friends, he did the gentlemanly thing and bowed out."

Not knowing what to say, her head and heart reeling, Rachel was hard-pressed to say much else but another "Oh."

"He'd kill me if he knew I was telling you all of this, it's just that—" she peeked over her shoulder to make sure they were alone "—I'm not getting any younger and the thought of having an instant grandson, as well as a daughter-in-law whose company I'm very much enjoying, fills me with indescribable joy."

CHANCE LOVES ME.

Lying in bed that night, listening to Wesley softly snore from the beautiful crib Chance had bought for him on a wondrously hectic shopping trip Tuesday afternoon, Rachel wasn't sure what to do with this knowledge.

Part of her wished Chance's mother had kept her nose out of her son's affairs. Another part, the part of Rachel increasingly craving Chance's touch, was secretly thrilled. But if she was falling for Chance, what did that say about her love for her poor husband? What kind of wife was she to so soon be falling head over heels for Wes's best friend?

Finding sleep impossible, she tossed back the covers and padded barefoot downstairs. Cookies and milk. That's all she needed to get this ridiculous notion from her head.

She *wasn't* falling for Chance. He was like her brother.

She was grateful to him.

"Hey, gorgeous," he said from in front of the open fridge, the dim light washing over the muscles of his bare chest. "Fancy meeting you here." He winked.

Her mouth went dry. That gratitude she was supposedly feeling for him? One sight of his rock-hard pecs and abs and there was no denying it. She wanted the guy—bad. Not in a friendly way, but in a way she had no business even thinking about, let alone aching to act upon.

"Um, hi," she mumbled, biting her lower lip.

"Want milk?" he asked, wagging the gallon jug.

"Yes, please."

While he poured, she grabbed the foil-wrapped plate of cookies from the kitchen's center island.

They reunited at the kitchen table.

"Why can't you sleep?" he asked.

For a long time, she stayed silent, toying with her cookie. "Truth? You."

Gracing her with a slow, sexy grin that turned her resolve to think of him as a brother to mush, he said, "I'm flattered. At least, I hope I have reason to be."

Swallowing hard, she nodded. Everything about him was good. So why, then, did the realization that she was falling for him hurt so bad?

"Rachel?" Setting his milk glass on the table, he asked, "You okay?"

In a last ditch effort to prove to herself—to both of them—that the two of them as a couple would never work, she blurted, "Kiss me."

Per Rachel's request, Chance did kiss her. At first, softly, reverently. But then, the closer she melded to him, the more he increased his pressure, dizzying her with fervent strokes of his tongue.

And then, just as abruptly as their kiss had begun, it ended with Chance pulling away.

Fingers sliding into the hair at his temples, breathing ragged, he said, "Sorry."

"For what?" she asked, eyes welling with emotion. "That was beautiful. It's been so long since I've felt anything but pain. Your kiss…it was as if somewhere deep inside me, the wall of grief I've been hiding behind has been shattered."

"That's all well and good," he said with a sharp laugh. "But what about Wes? Don't you feel guilty? As if our being attracted to each other is a betrayal of his trust?"

Eyes closed, she took a deep breath. "Honestly," she said, eyes open, facing Chance straight on, "I know how awful it must sound, but from the moment your lips touched mine, all I could think about was you."

TWO DAYS LATER, with Wes's life insurance check safely in the bank and her bills paid, Rachel should've been on top of the world. But as she finished wrapping the last of the presents she'd purchased for Chance and his family, all she really felt was sad. He'd invited her to stay with him through New Year's—longer if she liked—but after their kiss, she was more convinced than ever that maybe what would be best for them both was for her and Wesley to move on.

She'd already caused Chance so much trouble. Why stick around if their attraction would only bring him—not to mention, her—pain?

"You look pretty," he said from the living room door, hands behind his back.

"When's the last time you had your eyes checked? I'm a mess." From the oriental rug where she'd parked herself in front of the fire with a mess of bows, boxes and ribbons, she grinned up at him. Dressed in comfy, but hardly flattering sweats, her short hair sticking out at crazy angles and no makeup, she was sure she'd never looked worse.

"My eyes are fine," he said, wading his way through the mess. "Seeing you like this, so at ease in my home…it's my heart I'm worried about."

"Have you always been such a charmer?" she asked, batting her eyelashes exaggeratedly.

"I don't know, you tell me…" From behind his back, he withdrew a perfect cluster of mistletoe.

With him kneeling beside her, holding the sprig over her head, it would've been rude not to follow through with tradition. Seeing how she'd long since put Wesley to bed, Rachel had no qualms about reaching Chance halfway for a mesmerizing kiss.

"YOU KNOW," CHANCE said the next afternoon, Wesley gurgling high on his shoulders as they crunched their way through freshly fallen snow in the neighborhood's park, "at work this afternoon, I had some downtime while the jury was deliberating. I did some thinking."

"'Bout time," Rachel quipped.

Her sassy comment earned her a snowball fight. And like the day at the tree farm, the guys once again got the better of her. Laughing so hard her lungs burned from the cold, she cried, "Stop! I give up!"

"Oh, no," Chance said, setting a bundled Wesley beside him so he could tackle her with both hands. "You don't get to surrender until you apologize."

"Sorry, sorry," she laughingly cried, her foggy breath mingling with his.

He kissed her, and despite the fact they were lying

in the snow, she felt warmed inside. Which was wrong. She shouldn't be on fire for this man who was her husband's best friend.

"You're forgiven," he said a few minutes later, when her every defense had been shattered. "Now, back to what I was saying before you so rudely interrupted… I've been thinking about how you said you felt like you should find a place of your own. And then I got to thinking how much I enjoy having you both here. And how big this rambling old house of mine is for just me. And how Wes made me promise to look after you if anything should ever happen to him…"

Heart galloping like a herd of runaway reindeer, Rachel alternately dreaded, yet prayed for what she knew Chance would say next.

"And so, anyway, what would you think of the two of us getting hitched? You could still keep your own room, if that's what you wanted, but at least then it'd be official. Me watching out for you and Wesley, I mean."

Tears of joy and sadness stung her eyes.

"Well?" he asked while she blinked.

"Oh, Chance…" Holding her fingers to her mouth, she tugged off her fuzzy mittens with her teeth, then cupped her hand to his cold, whiskered cheek. "I would love nothing more than to marry you. If only there wasn't so much history between us…"

"Say no more," he said, pushing himself off her. "I understand." Snatching up Wesley, he trudged toward the house, telling her without a single word that he didn't truly understand—at all.

AFTER TURNING DOWN Chance's proposal, to say there was tension between them would've been a major understatement—which was why Rachel sat alone in the kitchen that quiet Christmas Eve morning, scanning apartment ads while Chance had gone off to work.

Sipping cocoa while Wesley crumbled a cookie in his high chair, she was startled when the doorbell rang.

"Chance?" she said, running for the front door, hoping now that he'd had time to think about it, he was okay with her suggestion that they remain just friends.

"Sorry," a well-dressed older man said, clearing his throat. "Are you Rachel Finch?"

"Y-yes." She fingered the pearls Helen had given her at her throat.

After introducing himself as Wes's old boss, he said, "Forgive me for dropping by, especially today of all days, but…there's no easy way to say this… we've, well…your husband's body has been identified. I thought you'd like to have his few personal effects."

WITHIN FIFTEEN MINUTES of Rachel's call, Chance roared his Jeep up his normally quiet street. Yes, he'd been deeply wounded by her turning down his proposal, but that didn't mean he was now going to let her down.

He heard the news through the office grapevine—and he also found out Franks had dropped by to pass the news along to Rachel. Chance fully planned to be by her side as she dealt with it all.

"You okay?" he asked, finding her alone at the kitchen table. She had opened the watertight pouch Wes had been using as a wallet the day he'd been shot. His gold watch, wedding band and the navy wallet all lay in front of her.

Wes had been the consummate Boy Scout, and he'd also hated boats. Back when they were kids, Chance kept a rowboat on his paternal grandparents' farm pond. One sunny afternoon when they'd been about ten, he and Wes had been out rowing when the boat capsized.

Wes didn't get upset often, but when his prized baseball cards fell in the water, he'd freaked—kind of like when he'd learned he was the only guy from the Portland marshal's office assigned to that unconventional-as-hell mission, trying to protect a witness who'd refused to leave his private island.

Had Wes known there was a chance he wouldn't be coming home?

"Rachel?" She still hadn't answered his question.

Looking shell-shocked, she nodded. "Yeah. I'm all right."

"Where's Wesley?"

"Down for his nap."

Pulling out the chair beside her, he asked, "You sure you don't want to be alone for this?"

She shook her head, and off they went on a journey down memory lane. Wes's driver's license and credit cards, photos and fast-food coupons—all of it was in pristine condition.

In the last pocket was a folded slip of yellow legal paper.

Hands trembling, Rachel opened it. "Oh, God," she said. "It's a note."

"'If you're reading this,'" she read aloud, "'then I'm so sorry, sweetie, but…'" She broke down. "I c-can't do this," she said. "Please, Chance. You read it."

He cleared his throat, continuing where she'd left off.

"'…but I've apparently croaked. I know, I know, right about now you're probably wanting to smack me for trying to find humor in this, but I suppose everybody's gotta go eventually, and unfortunately, it seems my time's up.

That said, you're not allowed to be sad— well, maybe you could mope a little for the first week, or two, but after that, I want to be staring down from Heaven at your beautiful smile. I want you having babies and good times and toasting me whenever the top's popped on a beer.'"

"You do this next part," Chance said, closing stinging eyes. "It's too personal."

She took the letter and read on.

"'By now, Chance has no doubt told you about the promise he made me to always watch over you. But what he probably didn't tell you is how he's always had a secret thing for you. Back when we first started dating, he was too much of a gentleman and friend to stand in the way of me marrying you. If I have died, Rachel, he'd be a good man for you. The best—

second only to me. Wink, wink. Be sure and give him a shot at…'"

She paused to catch her breath. "'…winning your heart.'"

Sobbing, Rachel clung to Chance, drinking in his goodness and kindness and strength.

"Shh…" Chance crooned, stroking her short hair.

"Even in death, he put my needs before his own," she said softly, gently setting the letter on the table. "And the timing…of all times for me to have finally gotten his letter, on Christmas Eve. What a gift. Makes you wonder if he's up there, watching over us."

"You doubted it?" Chance teased, sliding Rachel off her chair and onto his lap.

"After the rocky months I've had, I doubted not only Wes, but God."

"Gotta admit," he said, thumb brushing her lower lip. "Having you disappear on me like that—I've had my doubts, too."

"Yet look at us now," she said, resting her head on his shoulder. "Maybe Wes knew that without time and space between us, we'd have both been too loyal to his memory to give each other a try?"

"Whatever the reason," Chance said, "we don't have to feel guilty or pained anymore." He smiled at her, gently. "Now, with Wes's blessing, will you marry me, so that you, me and Wesley can start a family all our own?"

"What do you mean, *start*? I thought we already were a family?"

"Right," he said before a spellbinding kiss. "How could I forget?"

CHRISTMAS MORNING, WESLEY snug between them on the living room sofa, a fire crackling in the hearth and the scent of fresh-baked cinnamon rolls flavoring the air, Rachel opened gift after gift that Chance had secretly stashed in nooks and crannies all over the house.

Later, they'd go to his parents' for Christmas dinner with his sisters and extended family, but for now, it was just the three of them, opening sweaters and perfume and books and china figurines and fishing lures and hats and for Wesley, toys, toys and more toys—most of which Rachel guessed he wouldn't be able to play with until he was three!

Once they'd finished their gift extravaganza and all the wrappings had been cleared, Chance stood beside the Christmas tree and said, "Look, honey, here's another package in this bird's nest, and it's tagged for you."

"Chance," Rachel complained, heading his direction. "You've already given me too much."

"Look here, the label says it's from Santa," he said, holding out a tiny, robin's-egg blue box that screamed Tiffany.

Heart racing, hands trembling, Rachel lifted the lid to peek inside. "Chance…" Tearing at the sight of the glowing, pear-shaped diamond solitaire, she crushed him in a hug. "It's gorgeous. Yes, I'll marry you!"

"Whoa," he said with a sexy grin, pushing her back and shaking his head. "I don't recall asking anything. This was all Santa's doing."

"Well, then, *Santa*," she said, tilting her head back to talk to the high ceiling, "I accept your proposal."

"Now, wait a minute…" Chance pulled her back

into his arms. "Not so fast. I thought the two of us had reached an understanding. Those kisses you gave me last night implied a certain level of intimacy and trust. You can't just make out with me, then leave me for a big jolly guy in a red suit."

"Then what do you suggest?" she asked, standing on her tiptoes to press a kiss to his delicious, cinnamon-flavored lips.

"Just to be safe, you'd better marry me right away."

"Yeah, but do I get to keep the ring?"

He winked. "Why not? With any luck, Mr. Ho Ho Ho will go back to his wife…leaving me plenty of time under the mistletoe with mine."

* * * * *

COMING NEXT MONTH FROM

H HARLEQUIN®

American Romance®

Available November 3, 2015

#1569 LONE STAR TWINS
McCabe Multiples • by Cathy Gillen Thacker

Poppy McCabe and her best friend, Lieutenant Trace Caulder, marry in order to adopt twin infants, expecting their long-standing relationship to stay exactly the same. Instead, everything changes, including the two of them!

#1570 THE COWBOY'S CHRISTMAS FAMILY
by Donna Alward

Rancher Cole Hudson is determined to win the heart of Maddy Wallace, and her twin boys, too. But it'll take all his effort—and the spirit of Christmas—to thaw this beautiful widow's heart!

#1571 HER HOLIDAY RANCHER
Mustang Valley • by Cathy McDavid

Gabe Dempsey expected to inherit Dos Estrellas Ranch when his father died, but he didn't count on interference from Reese McGraw, the very attractive trustee of the estate—and the woman whose secret he's kept for twelve years.

#1572 THE SURGEON'S CHRISTMAS BABY
Cowboys of the Rio Grande • by Marin Thomas

Former army surgeon Alonso Marquez is afraid he won't be a good father, but Hannah Buck is determined to prove that her love is just what the doctor needs.

YOU CAN FIND MORE INFORMATION ON UPCOMING HARLEQUIN® TITLES, FREE EXCERPTS AND MORE AT WWW.HARLEQUIN.COM.

HARCNM1015

REQUEST YOUR FREE BOOKS!
2 FREE NOVELS PLUS 2 FREE GIFTS!

HARLEQUIN®

American Romance®

LOVE, HOME & HAPPINESS

YES! Please send me 2 FREE Harlequin® American Romance® novels and my 2 FREE gifts (gifts are worth about $10). After receiving them, if I don't wish to receive any more books, I can return the shipping statement marked "cancel." If I don't cancel, I will receive 4 brand-new novels every month and be billed just $4.74 per book in the U.S. or $5.49 per book in Canada. That's a savings of at least 12% off the cover price! It's quite a bargain! Shipping and handling is just 50¢ per book in the U.S. and 75¢ per book in Canada.* I understand that accepting the 2 free books and gifts places me under no obligation to buy anything. I can always return a shipment and cancel at any time. Even if I never buy another book, the two free books and gifts are mine to keep forever.

154/354 HDN GHZZ

Name	(PLEASE PRINT)	
Address		Apt. #
City	State/Prov.	Zip/Postal Code

Signature (if under 18, a parent or guardian must sign)

Mail to the **Reader Service:**
IN U.S.A.: P.O. Box 1867, Buffalo, NY 14240-1867
IN CANADA: P.O. Box 609, Fort Erie, Ontario L2A 5X3

Want to try two free books from another line?
Call 1-800-873-8635 or visit www.ReaderService.com.

* Terms and prices subject to change without notice. Prices do not include applicable taxes. Sales tax applicable in N.Y. Canadian residents will be charged applicable taxes. Offer not valid in Quebec. This offer is limited to one order per household. Not valid for current subscribers to Harlequin American Romance books. All orders subject to credit approval. Credit or debit balances in a customer's account(s) may be offset by any other outstanding balance owed by or to the customer. Please allow 4 to 6 weeks for delivery. Offer available while quantities last.

Your Privacy—The Reader Service is committed to protecting your privacy. Our Privacy Policy is available online at www.ReaderService.com or upon request from the Reader Service.

We make a portion of our mailing list available to reputable third parties that offer products we believe may interest you. If you prefer that we not exchange your name with third parties, or if you wish to clarify or modify your communication preferences, please visit us at www.ReaderService.com/consumerschoice or write to us at Reader Service Preference Service, P.O. Box 9062, Buffalo, NY 14240-9062. Include your complete name and address.

HAR15

SPECIAL EXCERPT FROM

Ⓗ HARLEQUIN®
™

American Romance®

Poppy McCabe and her best friend,
Lieutenant Trace Caulder, want to adopt twins and
raise them together—but they don't want to get married.
But it looks as if it's not up to them!

Read on for a sneak peek of
LONE STAR TWINS,
from Cathy Gillen Thacker's
McCABE MULTIPLES miniseries.

"You remember when you were home on leave two months ago?"

Hard to forget that weekend in Fort Worth. For two people who'd never been in love and likely never would be, they sure had amazing chemistry.

Oblivious to how much he wanted to hold her lithe, warm body in his arms and make sweet love to her all over again, Poppy persisted on her verbal trip down memory lane. "When we went to the Stork Agency and met Anne Marie?"

"Sure, I remember," Trace said, pausing to take in the sexy fall of Poppy's thick, silky mahogany hair. "Anne Marie was a nice kid." And at seventeen years old, Trace recollected, way too young to be pregnant. That was why she was giving up her children for adoption.

"Well, she's picked us to raise her twins!" Poppy exclaimed.

"Seriously?"

"Yes! Can you believe it?" She paused to catch her breath. "There's only one itty-bitty problem…"

Trace saw the hesitation in Poppy's dark brown eyes. Waited for her to continue.

She inhaled sharply. "She wants us to be married."

Whoa now. That had never been on the table.

Trace swung his feet off the desk and sat forward in his chair. "But she knows we're just friends—" and occasional lovers and constant confidantes, he thought "—who happen to want to be parents together." He thought the two of them had made that abundantly clear.

Poppy folded her arms in front of her, the action plumping up the delectable curve of her breasts beneath her ivory turtleneck. Soberly she nodded, adding, "She still gets that neither of us want to get hitched."

No woman prized her independence more than the outspoken Poppy. For a lot of very different reasons, he felt the same. "But?" he prodded.

"Apparently they didn't expect Anne Marie to choose us…but they wanted to give her a basis for comparison. As it turns out there was another couple that was also in the running, who Anne Marie's mother met and prefers, and they *are* married. But in the end, Anne Marie decided she wants us. On the condition," Poppy reiterated with a beleaguered sigh, "that we get hitched and the kids have the same last name."

Don't miss
LONE STAR TWINS by Cathy Gillen Thacker,
available November 2015 everywhere
Harlequin® American Romance®
books and ebooks are sold.

www.Harlequin.com

Copyright © 2015 by Cathy Gillen Thacker

HAREXP1015

Turn your love of reading into
rewards you'll love with

Harlequin My Rewards

**Join for FREE today at
www.HarlequinMyRewards.com**

Earn **FREE BOOKS** of your choice.

Experience **EXCLUSIVE OFFERS** and contests.

Enjoy **BOOK RECOMMENDATIONS**
selected just for you.

PLUS! Sign up now
and get **500** points
right away!

Earn
FREE
REWARDS
HarlequinMyRewards.com
Join
Today!

MYR16R

THE WORLD IS BETTER
WITH
Romance

Harlequin has everything from contemporary, passionate and heartwarming to suspenseful and inspirational stories.

Whatever your mood, we have a romance just for you!

Connect with us to find your next great read, special offers and more.

f /HarlequinBooks

🐦 @HarlequinBooks

www.HarlequinBlog.com

www.Harlequin.com/Newsletters

H HARLEQUIN®

A *Romance* FOR EVERY MOOD™

www.Harlequin.com

SERIESHALOAD2015